FOUR TALES
by
ZELIDE

MADAME DE CHARRIERE

FOUR TALES
by
ZELIDE

Translated by S. M. S.

LONDON
CONSTABLE & CO. LTD.
1925

PRINTED IN GREAT BRITAIN.
CHISWICK PRESS : CHARLES WHITTINGHAM AND GRIGGS (PRINTERS), LTD.
TOOKS COURT, CHANCERY LANE, LONDON.

*To the memory of PHILIPPE GODET,
by whose discrimination, art, and devoted
scholarship, Mme. de Charrière was first
restored to her place in eighteenth-century
life and letters.*

CONTENTS

vii

LIST OF ILLUSTRATIONS

INTRODUCTION

THE FOUR TALES HERE TRANSLATED HAVE, I
think, a dual interest. As literature they
possess a quiet but genuine merit, and fill a
graceful if inconspicuous niche in the cold temple
of eighteenth-century romance. But, also, to an
unusual extent they throw light upon their author,
and help to complete the picture of Madame de
Charrière, whose story, brought to light by the late
Prof. Godet, is briefly told in *The Portrait of Zélide*.

Madame de Charrière had many considerable
literary gifts, but invention was not one of them.
She drew directly on her own experience. The
background of her stories is the background of her
own life; the opinions of her heroines are her
opinions; their misfits her misfits. In life she was
proud and reserved; yet in her novels she told out
her secrets without compunction. Her fictions
stood like a transparent screen between her and the
world.

Madame de Charrière was born in 1740 of one
of the oldest families in Holland, a van Tuyll of
Zuylen. The first thirty years of her life were
spent in the towered and moated castle of Zuylen
or in the grave family house by a quiet canal in
Utrecht. Endowed by nature with a simple heart,
a sensuous temperament, and a mind of amazing

xi

alacrity, she was confined by the circumstances
of her birth in a society that was slow, stifling,
and heraldic. The rumour of her wit, her learning, and her unconventionality—qualities which
were viewed at home with critical apprehension
or affectionate dismay—spread beyond Holland,
where dowagers tossed their heads in disapproval,
to Voltaire at Ferney and the King of Prussia at
Potsdam, who both desired to attract her to their
courts. Alone by candlelight in the still room at
Zuylen she had her own occupations, writing
satires on Dutch society, studying Plutarch,
battling with physics and carrying on, for twelve
years, a clandestine correspondence with a rake.
Suitors were proposed to her: Dutch gentlemen
of breeding; she refused them. Some, who would
have served her turn, took flight. She turned
down Boswell, and rejected Lord Wemyss. And at
last she married her brother's Swiss tutor, a timid,
phlegmatic, stammering, and mathematical man.

From the cold dignity of Zuylen she found
herself transplanted to the sleep of Neuchâtel.
It was her own choice. Disdainful alike of worldly
advantage and intellectual display, she had reasoned
herself, under the influence of Rousseau, into the
simple life. It proved less simple than vacant.
The society on the shores of the lake feared her
and starved her mind. A husband who proved as

chilly as a fish disappointed, no less, her human and simple proclivities. Two sisters-in-law, one peevish and one pious, remained with her till her death, dividing between them the care of the house. Madame de Charrière lived, gallantly, in a perpetual void. Stoically, she sought to fill it by a ceaseless activity of the mind and pen. For a stretch of fifteen years she never took a walk outside the walls of her garden. A deep Dutch orderliness in her, which neither she nor others had suspected, attuned her habits, without reconciling her heart, to the circumstances of this life.

The distance between her and her punctilious husband widened, as the years passed, to a gulf. Childless, Madame de Charrière lived on at Colombier, a small band of dependents at her feet. She preferred to remain shut in her bedroom, playing the harpsichord, teaching Locke on the Human Understanding to her maid, writing and writing. The dream of literary fame that had haunted her girlhood was realized in *Caliste*. But the disillusion of life stole like a dry rot over her later books, "the bric-à-brac of her disenchanted mind."

Twice after her marriage she sought an outlet for the locked riches of her nature. She fell disastrously in love with an insignificant and handsome individual at Geneva, an episode which ended in humiliation and despair. Later, she centred her life on Benjamin Conſtant. This relation, perilous from a wide disparity in their ages, was made not less so by the excessive likeness of their natures. Eight years of an intimacy that was sometimes a torture had given her affeƈtion for Conſtant its moſt vital hold, when she saw him reft from her by Madame de Staël. Her life closed in. She wrote on, dryly, dead books, and died.

"But for whom can one write nowadays?" asked the Abbé de la Tour.

"For me," answered the young Baroness de Brenghen. . . .

"Lord, Madam! if only I could——"

"You could," interrupted the Baroness.

"No; I could not," said the Abbé. "My ſtyle would appear too insipid compared to that of the writers of to-day. Do people pause to observe a man who is merely walking when they are accustomed to seeing only mountebank tricks or acrobatic leaps?"

"Yes," said the Baroness, "people *do* pause to observe anyone who walks with sufficient grace and rapidity to a point of intereſt."

"Well! I will do my beſt," said the Abbé.

*   *   *   *   *

This little preamble to one of the later (and duller) of Zélide's novels would serve equally as a preface, or apology, for all of them. One must not look, in these leisurely and urbane trifles of the eighteenth century, for any originality of method, for sweep or speed in the action, or medical zest in the psychology. But Madame de Charrière was always able to cause the personages of her novels to " walk with sufficient grace " to some point of interest in their lives. And there she usually leaves them: and we may speculate as we will on the issue of Cécile's romance, the end of Mistress Henley's marriage, or the future of Caliste's unhappy love. The society has been described, the problem posed, the characters made clear; how it will all work out remains almost as uncertain in literature as in life.

For literature, at any rate the literature she made, was hardly a thing in itself, hardly an art or a vocation, but just a part of Zélide's life, an extension of herself—beyond the moat at Zuylen, beyond the *potager* at Colombier.

Family portraits and scutcheons, family genealogies, family parties, if one had to be serious about such things in company, at least one must laugh at them when alone. So, behind her locked door at Zuylen, she wrote *Le Noble*. The trifling satire —it is no more than a scenario—had a *succès de scandale.* Its authorship was not divulged, but it was more than suspected; and eyebrows were raised higher than ever when Zélide merrily entered the sedate drawing-rooms of Utrecht and The Hague. *Une demoiselle . . . cela!* And indeed, for a girl imprisoned in the stiffest Dutch society of the eighteenth century the satire was extremely audacious. The theme—that kind hearts are more than coronets—was less threadbare, it is only fair to remember, in 1760 than to-day. Its author would have been the last person to claim for this tale a serious literary merit; it is told with zest, and the figure of Baron d'Arnonville is rendered with a youthful and brilliant absurdity. But the interest of this first tale is frankly biographical rather than literary. *Le Noble* was an episode in— and an escape from—Belle de Zuylen's early life.

And then she escaped in earnest, by marrying the tutor. She was her own mistress at last, freed from the blank painted gaze of those framed ancestors, and the gaze, traditionally blank, of her living (but were they living?) relations. Rousseau's Switzerland proved disappointing, the vintage unclassical, the tasks of Nausicaa monotonous, the games of cards tedious, the gossip more tedious still. But to observe and note with skill and malice, until a work of delicate realism— the *Lettres Neuchâteloises*—had taken shape, that

was to use all this tedium to good effect. What
matter if the publication of this sketch made the
gossip more spiteful, and narrowed the available
society yet more? To be bored alone was always,
Belle thought, better than being bored in company.

But she was not alone; there was always
Monsieur de Charrière to reckon with. Blameless,
hesitating, pedantic, and unruffled, there he was.
And would be, to the end of the world; ever so
close, beside her. And Madame de Charrière,
shrinking from that cold ceaseless contact, from
those conventional maxims uttered with such
remorseless deliberation, from that tightness, that
impeccability, once more took refuge in a book.
She wrote *Mistress Henley*.

This novel was ostensibly an answer to a story
called *The Sentimental Husband* written by Samuel
Constant, the uncle of Benjamin, which exhibited
the misfortunes of a middle-aged husband un-
equally yoked with a gay young wife. In *Mistress
Henley* we are given the other side of the picture.
Although the book was published anonymously,
its authorship was an open secret. And though
the scene is laid in England and the circumstances
are disguised, no one at Neuchâtel had any doubt
as to the identity of the protagonists.

Some books are like shutters inadvertently left
ajar; they reveal, we are uncomfortably aware,

the author's private foible in a degree he does not measure or intend. In *Mistress Henley* the doors are flung wide. The writer lifts the curtains with the most disarming gesture, and " here," she says, " you may see just what happens—not through my husband's fault, certainly, nor wholly through my own—if a man of his character live with a woman of mine." What happens—what must inevitably happen: Madame de Charrière's attention dwells always on the rules of the human comedy, seeks impartially to discover them, delights in expressing them tersely, justly, without exaggeration or adjustment to her own case. If in her letters, or in this novel, she seems absorbed in her own reactions it is because these present themselves most readily and most fully for analysis. Her subject is human nature; she watches it in herself.

The story is " a pack of little things." Very deftly Madame de Charrière puts her heroine always in the wrong. Mr. Henley is credited only with one offence: that of being always and consciously and sadly in the right. " And all this for a cat to whom I have done no hurt! " said Mr. Henley, with a sad and gentle look, a look of resignation; and he went away. " No," I cried after him, " it is *not* the cat. . . ." But he was already far away." The story abounds with touches that Miss Austen would not have despised.

" Mistress Henley," wrote Zélide to a friend in Holland, " caused a schism in Geneva society. All the husbands were on Mr. Henley's side, many of the women on his wife's, while the girls did not dare to say what they thought. Never had fictitious personages seemed so much alive." Monsieur de Charrière read the book " with a sad and gentle look." Very carefully he read it, and tried to understand. But he could not apprehend that it was not the cat.

And in consequence of this crucial misapprehension he saw Madame de Charrière fall in love with a young gentleman at Geneva.

Mistress Henley was published in 1784, and in the same year Madame de Charrière printed the *Lettres de Lausanne*. The one deals with an actual, perhaps an indecently actual situation; the other with an imaginary one. In both she herself is speaking. And both are, like herself, refreshingly impersonal.

In the *Lettres de Lausanne* the scene is delineated with the same irony that in her first book caused such offence, to the citizens of Neuchâtel. Madame de Charrière never paid but the briefest visits to Lausanne. The tea-parties where Gibbon strutted and the clients of Dr. Tissot compared their ailments in all the tongues of Europe were not to her taste; and she watched with aloof amusement the efforts of the Swiss provincials to imitate the habits of a horde of French financiers, German princes with the colic, and English noblemen on the Grand Tour.

The story cast against this background is the tale of an inconclusive love affair between the *ingénue* Cecilia and a little English lord upon his travels, told in a series of letters from the girl's mother. The latter is, admittedly, Madame de Charrière herself. She advises her child with a directness and honesty which, we are told, shocked the prudish and sentimental ladies of the day, much as it might have offended Victorian mothers. Was it necessary, they asked, that a young girl should know that a suitor might sigh for her charms at the Governor's reception and yet embrace, that same evening, a woman of another sort? But the mind revealed in these letters is one of remarkable wisdom and charm; and Cecilia's dignity at the defection of the little Englishman to whom she had lost her heart is so unaffected, that we cannot be altogether unmoved when she is left to console herself in true romantic fashion with a pianoforte, a portfolio of prints, the care of a sick negro—the inevitable eighteenth-century negro—and of a starving dog. As in the *Lettres Neuchâteloises*, the provincial setting of the story is a truthful piece of *genre*; and the quiet light reflected on the writer may redeem the slender construction.

Cecilia—so the author told Monsieur de Salgas —was drawn, in her physical traits at any rate, from a certain Mademoiselle Röell. We must accept this statement; yet here too, I am convinced, there is an element of self-portraiture. If the mother is Madame de Charrière with her mature knowledge of human nature, Cecilia, by many touches, is Belle at the castle of Zuylen two years before the correspondence with d'Hermenches, when the candour and simplicity, so naively present beneath the brilliant surface of those letters, were still childish: wondering and waiting for life while the poplars flecked the unrippled moat with the slow sun.

Be that as it may, the relation between mother and daughter is drawn with an equally firm touch on both. It was a relation for which, as Monsieur de Salgas said, she had a born gift; and had the marriage with Charrière been fruitful, had there been a Cecilia at Colombier as well as a too real Mr. Henley, the tragic development of Madame de Charrière's nature would never have been played out.

The faith in education, characteristic of Rousseau's period, was hers to an almost pathetic degree. As a girl at Zuylen she had brought up her young brothers, teaching Plutarch to Vincent and life to the wide-eyed and romantic Dietrich. At Colombier we find her giving lessons in Locke to her maid Henriette, and some dim lights on Latin; the lifelong devotion of this unlikely pupil is a proof that her efforts, if misplaced, were not resented. Moreover, this Socratic energy, for ever goading the dormant minds around her to life, was coupled with a vigorous instinct of protection; and when Henriette, unregenerated by Locke, was compelled to concentrate her mind on an illegitimate baby, Madame de Charrière rose up with fine spirit as her champion against the persecution of the Calvinist community. In later years this protective instinct grew more masterful and pronounced; and Colombier became the centre of a strange band of curious dependents, exiles and eccentrics, whose wayward fortunes she guided and tolerated with a wise patience. But this, the richest vein in her nature, never found its obvious outlet.

There was no daughter to educate at Colombier; no one could educate Monsieur de Charrière. Inside the case which contained him his regulated mind irreproachably ticked. His clear complacency was without a crack. There was no Cecilia;—and we have *Caliste*.

Here the effort to disguise the personal confession is far more sustained than it was in *Mistress Henley*. But we have it from Benjamin Constant that the inspiration of this tale—the only tragic tale she wrote—was drawn from that mysterious episode at Geneva; and Madame de Charrière herself remarked, " I have never re-read *Caliste*: it cost me too many tears to write."

Zélide saw herself as Caliste; and Benjamin Constant, the most penetrating and critical of all her friends, has written, " To her who created Caliste and who resembles her." And yet nothing could well be more different from Madame de Charrière, as she presented herself to the world— a masterful, caustic blue-stocking, than the gentle heroine of this tale.

" Caliste is Madame de Charrière's hidden self: or, if you will, her anti-self. Caliste is made up, singly and limpidly, of all those emotions she knew she would have lived by, and had not. Zélide, at Zuylen, had sometimes revealed them ('But if I love . . . if I love,' she had written to Hermenches, the words starting like a jet from a smooth rock); but she had lost herself in the maze of her own mind: her sceptical and mocking reason. Yet, in the Portrait of Zélide, the features of Caliste are there behind the mask she was resolved to wear, and wore till the mask stiffened upon the face. Here, for once, she told it out. Caliste dies: it is the only one of her tales that can be said to have a con- clusion. She wrote *Caliste*, and never re-read it."[1]

[1] *The Portrait of Zélide.*

The book had an immediate success. Madame de Staël owns that but for it *Corinne* might never have been written. It was translated into English: it was the rage in Paris. Madame de Charrière had achieved her literary fame.

Yet in certain respects *Calisle* has stood the test of time less well than the earlier volumes. We shall look in it in vain for those truthfully observed details—those pieces of provincial *genre*—which give the *Lettres Neuchâteloises* and the *Lettres de Lausanne* their charm for any student of eighteenth-century life and manners who is willing to endure slowness of pace and slightness of incident for the sake of so entirely genuine a picture. *Calisle*, on the contrary, is a pure product of the Romantic Movement. It has all the improbable machinery and much of the high-flown sentiment which delighted the last years of the eighteenth century. Two infants are jumbled at birth; and the uncertainty as to which is the elder twin inspires in both of them a lifelong fraternal devotion with vows of perpetual celibacy in order that the rights of property may never be called in question. This is a bad beginning; or a good one, according to whether we are looking for a serious plot or prepared to enjoy an excellent " specimen " in the history of taste.

And, if the motive of literary curiosity is strong

enough to carry us through the conventional
romantic stock-in-trade which surrounds the
story, we shall be rewarded by the genuine pathos
and humanity of the central figure. For here
Madame de Charrière is writing once more of what
she knows. She never deceived herself, never
falsified her own emotions; and it is not difficult
to distinguish, beneath the occasional convention-
ality of the language of her time, the reality of
Caliste's tragedy.

And if her lover, with his endless vacillations
and Werther-like vapours remains unconvincing
to the end, the father, stupid, obstinate, upright,
and benevolent is old Monsieur de Tuyll to the life.
He cannot be made to act against his convictions,
and Caliste has no feelings of bitterness against him
for his firmness. Indeed, she has no bitterness at
all. Society is thus; facts are so. Is not this Zélide
herself? Ardent, seeking diligently for a happiness
that escapes her, never deceived by convention,
often mocking it, sometimes revolted by it; yet
in the bottom of her Dutch soul *ordentlyk* to the
last?

So she lived on at Colombier; writing, reasoning, protecting, and pretending that it was life.
Proudly reserved and scornfully resigned, she hid
all of her that was Caliste from the eyes of the
world and from her own. Pastor Chaillet, her

peering, inquisitive guest, divined it; Monsieur de Charrière dumbly apprehended it. But only Benjamin Constant was permitted to penetrate that screen, and scarcely forgiven for having done so.

When, after eight years, came the rupture with Benjamin, she sought in a first impulse of devotion to hold him at least by a literary sympathy. " I thought I would write new *Calistes* simply for your entertainment "—new romances shorn of " that bare style which you have blamed," romances in the manner of Madame de Staël. She returned to her books; but she never sought to make literature out of her broken friendship with Constant. Her books, thenceforward, are filled with theories, inspired by theories, not by life— her own, or anyone else's. They are Rousseau's theories in *Sir Walter Finch*, her own theories of democracy in *Les Trois Femmes*, political theories in *Les Emigrés* and half a dozen pamphlets. But never anything the least like life again. Her novels were only the extension of Zélide's personal life; and that, with the disappearance of Benjamin, was ended. Only her mind lived on, still seeking scornfully to follow the thread of Reason. Madame de Charrière's service of the eighteenth-century goddess was stoical to the last. Reason in books. Reason in human affairs. Was it enough? Had not the flame of her existence, the spark of it which endures in these few tales, been lent not by reason, but by something less logical, more humorous, more tragic, subtler—by life itself, which she had ardently longed for, and studied, and mistrusted, and renounced?

GEOFFREY SCOTT.

TRANSLATOR'S NOTE

*L*E NOBLE was probably first printed in 1763, *Mistress Henley* in 1784, *Lettres de Lausanne* in 1785, and *Caliste* in 1787. They are all, therefore, among the author's earlier works, and were selected together with the *Lettres Neuchâteloises* by Prof. Godet for republication at Geneva, a choice which any who may be led to attempt her later writings will readily approve.

In translating these tales I have endeavoured to keep as closely as possible to their author's text, and to retain the style and spirit of the period. But I have omitted one or two references to current books or local politics that only long footnotes would have rendered intelligible, and have ventured to abridge some moral reflections and financial details that appeared too tedious.

SYBIL SCOTT.

Het Huis te ZUYLEN, van den H.r Reynan Gerard
van. Huys van Serooskerken.

la Maison de ZUYLEN du Sr. Gerard van Tuyl
de Serooskercen.

THE NOBLEMAN

A TALE

THE NOBLEMAN

THERE ONCE STOOD IN ONE OF THE FRENCH provinces a very ancient castle, inhabited by an ancient scion of a yet more ancient family. Baron d'Arnonville—for such was his name—was exceedingly sensible of the value of all this ancientry, and in this he was wise, for he owned little else of value. Yet it would perhaps have been better if his castle had been a trifle less ancient, for one of its towers blocked up a portion of the surrounding moat while of the rest you could only perceive a little muddy water, where frogs had taken the place of fish. The Baron's table was frugal, but there hung all round the dining-hall the antlers of deer killed by his ancestors. He recalled on feast days that he had the right to shoot and on fast days that he had the right to fish. Thus, contented with the possession of these rights, he was enabled, without any sensation of envy, to permit his pheasants and his carp to be eaten by rich men of ignoble birth. He spent his modest revenues in bringing a lawsuit to prove his right to hang malefactors upon his property. It would never have occurred to him that it would have been possible to put his income to better account or to leave a more valuable heritage to his children than the power of executing justice. His private purse he employed to renew the escutcheons that bordered all his ceilings and to repaint the portraits of his ancestors.

3

Baroness d'Arnonville had been dead for many years and had left him one son, and one daughter, named Julia. The young gentleman might, with good reason, have complained equally of his character and his education, but in fact he complained of neither. Content with the name of d'Arnonville and the knowledge of his family tree, he dispensed easily both with talent and knowledge. Occasionally he shot, and ate his game in the company of the young woman of the neighbouring tavern; he drank heavily and gambled every evening with his lackeys. His person was unpleasing, and keen eyes would have been needed to discern in him those characteristics which, according to some, are the infallible signs of noble birth. Julia, on the contrary, was endowed with beauty, charm, and intelligence. Her father had obliged her to read some treatises on heraldry that had not entertained her, and she, herself, had read in secret some romances which had entertained her exceedingly. A visit she had paid to a lady of her family in the capital of the province had given her some knowledge of the world; much is not required to render a person genteel who has an observant mind and a generous heart.

A painter, who had been employed to copy her ancestors and their quarterings, had once given her some drawing lessons; she could depict landscapes and embroider flowers. She sewed with skill and sang with taste, and as her person had need neither of art nor magnificence, she was

4

always held to be well dressed. She was vastly vivacious and merry, although tender, and jests on the subject of nobility had been known to escape her, but the respect and friendship she felt for her father had always kept them within bounds. Her father reciprocated her love but he would have preferred her to embroider armorial bearings rather than flowers, and to study the mouse-eaten parchments that enumerated his family titles rather than to read *Télémaque* and *Gil Blas*. It vexed him to observe that modern engravings hung near to the window in her room while the old portraits were banished to a dark recess, and he often scolded her for preferring some pretty and amiable girl of the middle class to a young noblewoman of the neighbourhood, who was both plain and sullen. Moreover, he would have liked her to give place only to rank, according to the dates of creation, and Julia never consulted Patents of Nobility, but gave place always to age, and would rather have been thought plebeian than proud. From thoughtlessness she might have walked out before a princess, from indifference or civility she might have let everyone precede her.

She did not pretend to excessive cleverness, so that what talents she possessed gave all the more pleasure. She knew very little, but one saw that it was because she had not had the opportunity of learning; her ignorance never bore the appearance of stupidity. Her lively, sweet, and smiling countenance attracted all who beheld it, and her

gracious manner completed the prepossession her
physiognomy had caused. She had become a
great favourite with a Parisian lady whom she had
met at her relative's house, and this lady now
invited her to stay at her country seat. Julia
succeeded in obtaining her father's consent, and,
after he had counselled her never to forget her
rank, he permitted her to depart. Her hostess was
very wealthy and had an only son, who was, nevertheless, both amiable and well brought up. He
was personable, Julia was pretty; they pleased
each other at first sight and did not, at the beginning, think either to show or to conceal their
feeling. Soon, however, they let it be understood, and found each other all the more amiable
when assured of pleasing. In company, at table,
or when walking, Valaincourt would murmur or
hint some tender thought to Julia; but, as soon as
they were alone and they might have spoken
freely, he ceased to address her. She was surprised at this and yet satisfied; either she had read
or had divined that love is timid when it is ardent
and delicate, and although no speech would have
pleased her like her lover's, she was equally happy
in his silence.

Valaincourt had, however, in addition to the
reasons that Julia surmised, a further reason for
silence that she did not know. She had seen that
he had fine eyes, fair hair, and beautiful teeth; she
had found in him sweetness, intelligence, and
generosity, and she had remarked order, decency,

and opulence in his home. But she had forgotten to enquire which of his ancestors had been ennobled. Unluckily it was his father, who, by distinguished services and many virtues, had merited this honour. Wise men might argue that when rank has been acquired in this manner the most recent nobility is the best, that the first noble of his race has the most right to be proud of a title which he has won for himself, that its second bearer will be worth more than its twentieth, and that it is to be presumed that Valaincourt resembled his father more closely than Baron d'Arnonville his thirtieth ancestor. But wise men are not competent to judge the work of prejudice, and Valaincourt knew of the prejudice and the weight it would have with Julia's father.

But now the date for Julia's departure was at hand; and the distress of the lovers increased their tenderness.

At the moment of retiring for the night they chanced to find themselves alone in an unlit corridor. Valaincourt took Julia's hand and kissed it with more emotion than he had yet shown (for it was not the first time that he had kissed it, and Julia, during the past few days, had always removed her glove before giving her hand to Valaincourt). The following day they found themselves in the same corridor and the same darkness; whereupon Valaincourt kissed Julia, and Julia, who did not like to refuse what she could so easily grant, let herself be kissed. The day after Julia went expressly to the corridor, but found it lighted; Valaincourt extinguished the light and kissed her tenderly—then kissed her again Julia would have liked to return his kisses. . . . Luckily it was the last evening. The next morning she departed.

So long as she was able to be with Valaincourt she had thought only of the joy of seeing him and of hearing him speak, but when it was not in her power to see him she commenced to feel the pangs of separation and to desire some way of seeing him again and of seeing him for ever. One cannot know precisely what she thought or felt, but, fortunately, the young man thought and felt the same.

One day, as she sat alone over her embroidery, Valaincourt entered. She remembered the incident of the corridor and coloured, but Valaincourt did not appear to remember it, such was the respect with which he approached her. A woman whom a man esteems and who has modest and decent manners may often thus cause him to doubt the very favours that she has bestowed. Valaincourt could not believe that his lips had dared to touch the countenance of this goddess.

After the first exchange of civilities he relapsed into silence. Julia, who did not any longer believe herself inaccessible, thought they had seen enough of each other to be no longer so reserved and that he should have been able to divine some part of her feelings. She therefore grew vexed at his silence. " In his place," she said to herself, " I should have spoken." Simultaneously she rose to ring the bell, and, as the lackey entered, she said to Valaincourt, " You are very polite to have come so far since you have nothing to say to me." Then, to the servant, " Some coffee, if you please, and, if my father is at home, tell him to come and drink it."

" Ah, Mademoiselle," replied Valaincourt, " it is not easy to speak when I reflect that on what I say may depend all our future happiness or misery. I might speak amiss. Good God! I might not choose the right words with which to persuade you. Julia, my beloved Julia, tell me what I ought to say. What words, what inducements, what promises would persuade you to give your-self to me? "

" Oh, Valaincourt! " said Julia, with a look and a smile that promised everything, that said " yes," to all that he would have desired to ask.

Valaincourt, who understood, asked for nothing more. Beside himself with joy he seized her hands and kissed them in rapture, he even dared, he dared in broad daylight to press his lips upon hers; her father might at any moment have entered but they were heedless of danger; what danger indeed could they have feared in that moment of ecstasy! It was but brief, however; Julia quickly took fright both at her lover's ardour and her own complaisance.

" Let me go, Valaincourt," she cried, " we are forgetting ourselves."

At that instant they heard a sound and hastened to their seats. Julia bent her head over her work to conceal her disorder, while the young man went forward to meet Monsieur d'Arnonville with an air of timidity that appeared to prepossess that gentleman in his favour.

" I have taken, sir, the liberty of coming to visit your daughter, with whom my good fortune has made me acquainted."

" Have you never then seen my castle? "

" No, sir; I never had any excuse for paying you my respects."

" It is worth seeing," said the old gentleman, " a Baron d'Arnonville whose great-grandfather had been knighted by Clovis built it in 456. It is therefore not surprising that he had it made as spacious as you perceive it to be, for, at that time, nobility was respected as it should be. It was wealthy and powerful and was also rarer and purer than it is nowadays. Now it is only an ordinary recompense, and I, for one, think nothing of all these little nobles without ancestors."

" *We* have ancestors," remarked Julia, " from the garret down to the cellar."

" And most, even of the most ancient families," pursued the Baron, " have been contaminated through their alliances; there are very few, I think I may say, who have remained, like the d'Arnonvilles, entirely unsullied. I therefore hope that my children——"

" Undoubtedly," broke in the young man, who

could bear no more, "undoubtedly there is an added satisfaction and motive for virtue in finding among one's ancestors examples only of virtue and patriotism, and when high merit is added to a great man, and, in place of vanity——"

"As you have never seen the castle," went on the Baron, "you can never have seen the portraits. I will show them you, for that cannot fail to be useful to you in your historical studies. Will you follow me, sir?"

"Will your daughter not accompany us?" asked Valaincourt in a tone of dejection.

"No," replied Julia laughing, "I have lived enough among my grandparents to know them very well."

Valaincourt disconsolately followed the Baron, who, as the young man pleased him, did not spare him one portrait, one coat of arms, or one anecdote. And not a portrait, not a coat of arms but called forth some observation that touched Valaincourt to the quick. It was not that he was humiliated by such absurd ostentation, for he would not have had his nobility date from King Ninus at the cost of being as vain and foolish as the Baron. But, Julia. . . . At last he entered her room, trembling with emotion. While the father embroiled himself in the history of the first of his ancestors, Valaincourt hastily examined the work of the daughter. He saw on a table one finished landscape and one that she had just begun, and, among her brushes and colours, he discovered a little catechism, Segrais, Racine, and *Gil Blas*. He saw the fine engravings that she had preferred to the old portraits, he saw her flowers. . . . But of all the rest he saw nothing once he had caught sight of Julia's portrait. It was a pencil sketch and a good likeness. Valaincourt now thought of nothing but distracting her father's attention.

"Who is that respectable gentleman?" he asked, "there, behind you, sir."

The Baron turned.

"It is he of whom I have just been speaking at such length; did you not hear?"

"Yes, sir; forgive me. Now I recollect."

Valaincourt had the portrait safe and desired nothing more, but, seeing that the father was beginning again, he also took the landscape, which was to his taste. At length they left the room.

"Is it not true," enquired Julia, when they had rejoined her, "that I am rich in grandfathers? My grandmothers are not handsome but that does not signify; they are ancient. I intend to be painted many times, plain or handsome, for in three hundred years my portrait will be worth its weight in gold."

"Ah, Mademoiselle," replied Valaincourt, "your portrait will never be worth as much as it is to-day, vanity may perhaps venerate it in times to come, but love now adores it!"

"Have you then seen it, sir?"

"Yes; you will discover that I have indeed seen it; I have also seen your books and your paintings."

" Did it not divert you to see my ancestors? "

" No, Mademoiselle, I only had eyes for what concerned you." All this was said in a low voice. Julia smiled, and Valaincourt was pleased to remark that the daughter did not have the same respect for antiquity as the father.

It grew late and Valaincourt had to take leave. . . .

" Is that young man in love with you? " asked the Baron.

" I think so, father."

" Does he wish to marry you? "

" Yes, father."

" Is he of noble birth? "

Julia did not know, but supposed so and said " yes," once more.

" Of an ancient family? "

" Yes, father."

" From whom is he descended? "

" From Renaud de Montauban," answered Julia, more from a spirit of mischief than from any desire to deceive.

" What! my dear child; from Renaud de Montauban! Lord! how happy you will be! What felicity for me to see you make such a marriage! "

On saying this he embraced her with embarrassing tenderness. She immediately repented of having deceived him in a matter that appeared to him of such importance, and feared the consequences of her pleasantry. She also felt revolted

13

by such folly; and these contrary sentiments caused her so much agitation that she found herself obliged to retire to her room.

She sat down, leaned her arms on her toilet table, and pressed her head on her hands. " My father," she thought, " does not inquire if Valaincourt's heart is good or his character estimable; he asks only if his family is ancient. On that assurance he gives me to him. . . . Now, should Valaincourt prove *not* to be noble he will refuse him my hand and will be all the more implacable because I have deceived him. Good God! How foolish, how wicked have I not been! "

After a little more musing in the same sad vein she rose, and, pacing up and down her room, turned to distract herself by looking at the painting of which Valaincourt had spoken. Not finding it in its place she looked for her portrait. . . . Then she understood what Valaincourt had meant and how his theft had appeared to him equally pleasant and gallant. She pictured her father saying, " There is Jean-François-Aléxandre d'Arnonville," while Valaincourt was reflecting, " Here is Julia d'Arnonville, how can I carry her off? " When a young girl feels herself to be tenderly loved her sorrows are quickly lightened, for such a reason for happiness disposes the heart to gaiety. Julia now reflected that, even if Valaincourt did not descend from Renaud, he certainly must descend from someone else, that it might be possible to pass off her deception as a mistake, indeed that it might even be possible to turn it to good account by warning Valaincourt and concocting a genealogy with him.

"If reason has no weight with my father," she thought, "is it not possible to deceive him a little? Need we become victims of so absurd a prejudice?"

This rather easy morality suited her and she ceased reflection. It then occurred to her to write a warning to Valaincourt, and she took her portfolio, her pens, and her paper. She pondered over the means of conveying her letter to him, and I swear that she would indeed have written had she been sure of her style or her spelling. But she passed rapidly over these reasons for not writing and proceeded to persuade herself, while putting away all this apparatus, that prudence, reserve, modesty, and respect for propriety alone had checked her. She then congratulated herself on the very virtues that she did not possess. Soon she was called to supper, where her father, who had already confided his hopes to his son, could hardly restrain his talk before the servants. When these were dismissed they drank to the health of Renaud's descendant, and Julia, unable to support the spectacle of their satisfaction, withdrew once more, equally ashamed of her own imprudence and their absurdity. Once alone in her chamber she began to cry. Love, remorse, fear, and hope by turns confused and oppressed her. When a girl is agitated by conflicting emotions and does not know how to extricate herself, she usually weeps.

When Julia had ceased to weep her distress had abated; little, indeed, of her emotion remained but the idea of her lover. She beheld him as he had appeared to her at the first moment of their meeting, she recalled every token of his affection, and she reproached herself alternately with having responded with too much freedom for propriety or too much reserve for love. At length she went to bed, reflecting that it appeared a very long time since she had seen her couch.

" Was it really only this morning," she thought, " that I got up? Was it only after dinner that Valaincourt came? " No previous day had ever appeared to her so long, because no day had ever been packed with so many agitating sensations. She could hardly believe that, in so brief a space of time, she had felt and thought so many different things, or experienced so much joy and sorrow. . . . Despite her emotion she slept soundly and her dreams prophesied no evil. On the following day she was troubled by no presentiments and passed half the morning painting in her room. Her father was dining at a neighbouring castle, so she was alone. How many times did she not wish that Valaincourt might appear and put these idle moments to some good use!

Having seated herself after dinner on a bench in the avenue she saw Valaincourt approach—but in her father's company. During the forenoon he had sat, gazing at his mistress's portrait, but now he wished to see his mistress herself. He had set

16

out on this errand immediately after dinner, but
had met Monsieur d'Arnonville, who was on his
way home. The Baron did not delay speaking of
the subject that was uppermost in his mind.

"I have learned, sir," he said, after many low
bows, "I have learned that you love my daughter
and wish to marry her."

Valaincourt, confounded, only replied to this
opening by another low bow. Astonishment and
anxiety were depicted on his countenance and
struck him dumb.

"My fate is now to be decided," he thought.
"Good God! What is he about to say?"

"I had long decided," went on the Baron in a
gracious manner, "only to give my daughter to a
man of illustrious birth; the d'Arnonvilles could
bring dishonour to no family, they might aspire to
anything; my ancestors——"

"Ah, sir," imprudently interrupted Valaincourt, "I am aware of all your superiority; I know
that I am not worthy of your alliance; but if the
tenderest love and the most lively desires to give
happiness to your charming daughter could weigh
with you against the claims of birth, if honour,
honesty, devotion to you, yourself——"

At that moment Julia drew near. She had heard
what Valaincourt was saying and her confusion
explained the mystery. He was standing in such a
way as not to see her, but her father was no longer
paying any heed to him. He cast on his daughter
a look that brought her to her knees. Valaincourt,

perceiving this movement, gazed, astonished, at the pair, quite unable to divine the cause of so touching a scene. He did not know what to think or to say. Julia, her eyes bent on the ground, wept silently. Her father, furious, was incapable of speaking. At length, recovering his voice, he cried, " Unworthy child! You intended then to deceive your father? Was all that you told me of your lover's birth a fable? "

" Oh, father," answered Julia. " I, indeed, am guilty, but not Valaincourt——"

" What, Julia," cried her lover, " so I have betrayed you. I ought to have guessed, I ought to have kept silence. . . . You erred for my sake, and I have betrayed you. Sir," he continued, now on his knees beside Julia, " Sir, pardon a fault that was caused by love and of which we both therefore are guilty. Permit me to love your daughter, although her wit, and her beauty, as well as her birth, raise her high above me. She indeed deserves a throne, but no king could love her more tenderly; she could never find more tenderness than in my heart, she could never be more truly worshipped. Once again I pray you to permit me to love her, to see her, and to see you, so that your own judgment can decide our fate."

" Renaud de Montauban! " murmured Julia's father, as if he had heard none of this. Then, "For how many years has your family been noble?"

Valaincourt made no reply.

18

" Speak," said Julia, " and be honester than I was."

" Thirty-five years."

" Thirty-five years! And you aspire to my daughter's hand! Go, mademoiselle; go and weep for your shame, and do not venture to appear again before me. And you, sir, never let yourself be seen here again! Get at once out of my sight," he continued to Julia, who still knelt, weeping, beside him. " I could not have believed that you would have forgotten your birth to this degree. You little deserve to be what you are! "

" Undoubtedly," said Valaincourt, as he assisted Julia to rise, " Undoubtedly she did not deserve a father like you."

He would have said more had a look from Julia not silenced him. While she took, still weeping, the road to the castle, her lover withdrew, cursing all the nobility and his own ill-fortune.

As for the Baron, outraged, insulted, and so overcome that he could not walk, he seated himself on the same bench where, a few minutes previously, Julia had been lost in peaceful reverie. He caused a man, who was working in the garden, to summon his housekeeper and, having told her the story in a few words, instructed her to see that Julia did not leave her room or receive news of her lover. This housekeeper was, herself, one of the antiquities of the castle, and as, ever since her distant childhood, she had heard and seen nothing but the folly of her masters, she had almost as lively a sense of aristocracy as the Baron himself. She therefore entered wholeheartedly into his feelings, and ran willingly to shut up her young mistress. Julia, although by nature docile, grew indignant at such harsh treatment, and when the old woman, having explained her mission, began, "For a young lady of your rank——"

"Be silent," she said, "I have had enough of this nonsense. Lock the door if you like, but go."

For the next two days Julia refused either to listen or speak; she ate very little, slept scarcely at all, and wept incessantly.

Meanwhile the Baron, left alone on his bench, had reflected. "A petty, newly created nobleman to presume to alliance with me, and my daughter to listen to him! On part of the one what audacity, of the other what ignominy!" He repeated this to himself until nightfall; he then said it to his son; he said it at night in his dreams, and, the following morning, on making the round of the portraits, he thought to see in their looks indignation and reproach. On the third day, when the wind blew down into a muddy ditch a portion of the pigeon-cote with the weather-cock bearing the d'Arnon-ville arms, his mind was overcome with fear. He retired to bed, sick with apprehension, and scarcely had he fallen asleep when he beheld the ghosts of his ancestors, with visages of horror and armed to the teeth, surround his bed. He woke with a start and begged them rather to appear to his daughter, but the antique shades did not obey him. Julia,

who had that very evening received a note from
Valaincourt, slept peacefully; *her* dreams were born
of love and hope.

Valaincourt, in order to send her this note, had
bethought him of the gardener's daughter, to
whom Julia's kindness had attached her. This girl
willingly undertook the errand and prayed permission of the old housekeeper to carry some fruit
to Julia. Madame Dutour, who, at heart, was not
unkind, and who had commenced to feel pity for
her mistress's distress, consented, and the girl, after
chatting a little with Julia, whispered to her that
she would find a letter at the bottom of the basket.
No sooner was Julia alone than she found it. This
was what she read:

" BELOVED AND LOVING JULIA,

" Since you, also, have the power of love, I
need not tell you all that I am feeling and suffering.
Indeed, how could I find words to describe it?
My design is rather to assure you that there is
nothing that I would not undertake, nothing that
I would not venture to deliver you from the
cruel hands that thrust us apart. . . . It is not
possible that you will not consent; it is not
credible that you can share your father's ridiculous
prejudice. If I thought this, if I believed for one
moment that you might repent, that you might be
less happy, God knows how willingly I should
renounce all my own happiness. Tell me, Julia,
have you any such fears? My birth. . . . No,

forgive me; I know you love me and I must not
doubt your love. You could not hold unworthy
of your hand him whom you believe worthy of
your tenderness. Is it not for me that you are
suffering? Trust to my love, beloved Julia, and
you will not suffer long."

Julia somehow believed this without having any
solid reason for her faith. She read and re-read the
charming letter, and, as she read it, hope and even
happiness reawakened in her heart. She ate, she
slept, and, the following day, she went back to her
work and her painting.

Madame Dutour found her gentle and affable as
before, and at last had the satisfaction of lecturing
her without interruption. The next day the little
girl came back with her basket, just as Madame
Dutour was saying, " With your birth you might
aspire to the greatest match."

" It is very probable," answered Julia, smiling.

" Your husband might be a great nobleman and
you might then have a great castle and be very
happy."

" It is very possible," replied Julia, in an even
gentler and gayer tone.

Madame Dutour, thinking to have made good
progress, departed to congratulate herself and to
inform the Baron that he had only to wait and to
let her work in order to see Julia in two more days
quite forgetful of her love. Unluckily she found
no one to whom to communicate either her success

or her satisfaction for the Baron had gone out, in order to distract his mind, leaving word that he would only return the following day. Julia, meanwhile, hastened to avail herself of the housekeeper's absence in order to read Valaincourt's letter. He told her that, after examining everything, he judged her escape to be easy, her window being low and the portion of the moat below it being almost dry. He himself would meet her in the avenue at midnight, and a light coach would carry them before daybreak to a neighbouring town, where they could swear to their eternal fidelity at the altar steps. " I no longer doubt my happiness," he continued, " for now that it depends only on you, dearest Julia, doubt would be an insult to you. Love has given you to me and his rights are sacred. At midnight, when the moon has begun to disperse the shadows, quit the barbarous prison where prejudice has confined you, and let Love lead you to your lover's arms. I ask no answer, for you have confessed that you love me, and, in that confession have promised everything. At midnight then, Julia . . . what a moment, what ecstasy! "

Julia dropped the letter and remained for some time immobile. A feeling, composed both of surprise and joy, such as the unexpected appearance of an agreeable but wholly novel object awakens in us, held all her faculties in suspense. An elopement! That very night! To leave her father's house and give herself to Valaincourt! At length she rose, opened the window and, without admitting her intention to herself, looked to see if indeed it would be easy to escape. Seeing that, on that head, there was no objection to be made, she picked up the letter and read it again.

" It is true," she thought, " that the prejudice which holds me here is as barbarous as it is absurd. It is true that I said I loved him . . . Valaincourt does not doubt of my consent, to do so, he says, would be an insult to me. I am his . . . he will expect me. . . ."

The very same tone of authority that renders a husband so odious, how attractive is it not in a lover? In the same manner as the rights of the one are diminished because they are hated, so are those of the other magnified because they are beloved. Liberty is no longer desired when it wars with desire; had Valaincourt implored, had he asked timidly for Julia's consent, he might never have obtained it, but he commanded, and she thought herself unable to disobey. Valaincourt might perhaps have found it difficult to explain those sacred rights of love which he had claimed with such confidence. But Julia asked neither for explanation nor proof, but believed his word and thought herself to be less influenced by her passion than by some inviolable duty, which she, herself, did not wholly comprehend. Behold her, therefore, almost resolved! She shed a few tears as she thought of the father she was abandoning and of the home in which she had been born, in which she had grown up and which she was about to leave. But then she thought of her lover and dried her eyes.

" I shall be his," she thought, " I shall be his for ever."

Then she went back to the window, and looking, with closer attention, observed that at the very spot where she would have to descend, there was a hollow filled with the day's rains. This hollow must be filled. What could she use? Julia looked round and perceived the portraits of her ancestors.

" You can do me at least this service," she cried.

And, laughing, she jumped on a chair in order to detach " Jean-François-Aléxandre-d'Arnon-ville." Grandpapa was thrown down into the mud, but he was not enough, so was followed by a second ancestor, then by a third. Never had Julia thought to put her forefathers to such good use!

This performance diverted her. Nevertheless she was still much agitated, and if, on the one hand, her heart rejoiced at the thought of being her lover's, on the other it bled for her father's sorrow. Ah! if only the principles of a good education could then have influenced a mind that was naturally virtuous and still unformed. But the arguments for duty that her father had always employed were even less sound than those that her lover now advanced in the cause of love.

The little girl came back to fetch her basket; not knowing the purport of the letters she carried she had yet perceived that a reply from Julia gave great happiness to Valaincourt, so she enquired if there were any orders for her.

Julia hesitated. This was the moment to destroy Valaincourt's hopes. She grew pale; she blushed.

" No," she said at length in a trembling voice. Then she made a present to the child.

At eight o'clock her brother paid her a visit; it was his first. After some not too delicate raillery he recounted to her how he had honoured a little *parvenu* by playing with him at a game which he, himself, knew very well, and the other not at all, and how, enchanted by finding such a dupe, he had played all day and won a considerable sum. One never judges a fault of which one is incapable more severely than when one's conscience is burdened with some other sin. Julia accordingly told him that his conduct was shameful and cowardly; he made a scornful reply and took his leave.

" I shall soon be rid of all this charming nobility," she thought. " Why, I might have been condemned to pass my life with somebody like him, and people would have thought me happy if he had had sufficient quarterings. . . . Oh, let these great gentlemen become Knights of Malta or of any other noble order, for that is their birthright; Valaincourt will offer no objection and will give up to them, without jealousy, both the honour and the vows; but my heart and hand have nothing to do with such decorations."

She went on with her preparations for escape until her housekeeper had brought her supper;

26

then she went to bed in order that no suspicions might be aroused. When all were sleeping, from the young Baron to his favourites, the hounds, she rose and dressed herself in the darkness and without a mirror, thinking that, by night and the pale light of the moon, Valaincourt would hardly divert himself by examining her toilet.

The moon shone out, midnight sounded, Julia threw from the window a package of her favourite treasures, climbed herself on to the window-sill, descended, then climbed up again. . . . Something seemed to be holding her back—she seemed to hear her father speak, . . . but what does he say to her? He speaks of her name, her birth, the rank which it is for her to maintain! It did not seem to Julia that any of these considerations affected her closely, or that there was any good reason for her to be less happy than her waiting-maid—to whom an elopement would seemingly be permitted. Love proffered less feeble arguments and resolved her. She jumped down heavily on to the face of one of her ancestors. It broke under her feet. The noise awoke the housekeeper, who slept near by. But thinking it was merely caused by one of the ghosts who had the habit of haunting the castle, she contented herself with murmuring an " Ave Maria " and burying herself once more in her counterpanes. So, for once, the ghosts were of some use.

Julia advanced through the ruins and entered the courtyard. A dog stirred but did not betray her. She intended to pass out by a little door but, by ill-luck, found it closed. She retraced her steps, trembling. "Good God! what shall I do if I find no way out?" she murmured. But only a low wall barred her way, she climbed over it, she reached the avenue, she was with her lover. . . .

Let us not trouble ourselves any more about them!

The following day, when the terrible news was broken to the Baron, he fell, senseless, to the ground. On coming to himself, after much time and many remedies, he murmured in a half audible voice, "A newly created nobleman! Oh, my ancestors! oh, the disgrace!"

It was feared that he would die of chagrin. In vain did a sensible man who was with him represent that, at the most, nobility afforded but a presumption of merit and that when, as in Valaincourt's case, merit was recognized, there was no need of the presumption; also that no one could take credit for the merit of someone else and that, even were that possible, a nobleman would be no better off than another as the ancestor to whom he owed his title might easily have been a rogue or a fool. . . . This blasphemous discourse was cut short by a second swoon, even longer than the first.

Indeed it would, I think, have been all over with the Baron if a very consoling letter had not brought him back to life. Fate had recompensed him for the acquisition of an agreeable son-in-law by offering him the most disagreeable daughter-in-law conceivable. This compensation he accepted with joy. He gave thanks to heaven and admired the wisdom of Providence which dispenses equally both good and evil. It is not necessary to say that the young lady was immaculately noble; her portrait was not sent to him, but her genealogical tree was, and it was such that the father did not for an instant hesitate. The son had heard that the lady had a squint and a humpback, but the honour of joining her arms and quarterings with his caused him to pass lightly over these inconveniences. Moreover, he reckoned on consoling himself with women less noble and less ill-favoured; for he had too much grandeur of soul to think it necessary to love the lady whom he espoused. The marriage, therefore, was soon concluded.

Julia, when she heard the news, had herself informed of the wedding day. At the end of the banquet the Baron, remembering the vigour of his youth, celebrated so well-assorted a union in twenty bumpers. When the wine had commenced to cause some confusion in his wits concerning ancient and modern nobility, Valaincourt and Julia entered the hall and threw themselves at his feet. Having lost a portion of what he called his reason he felt only tenderness and granted them forgiveness. Julia was happy, and her sons were not Knights of Malta.

MISTRESS HENLEY

MISTRESS HENLEY

LETTER I [1]

WOULD IT BE AGREEABLE TO YOU, CHILD, if I were to narrate to you the history of my marriage and of all that led to it, afterwards describing to you my life as it is to-day? I shall be compelled to tell you some things which you already know in order that you may understand others of which you are in ignorance. Let me explain to you the notion that has come to me. If my letter, or my letters, contain any truth and appear to you likely to excite any interest, if only sufficient to cause them to be read, I will give you leave to translate them, merely altering the names and omitting what appears to you to be tedious or unnecessary. I believe many women to be just in my case. I should like, if not to effect a change in, at least to offer a caution to husbands; I should like to put things in their proper places and to give everyone his due. I feel indeed a slight scruple over my project, but it is *very* slight. I have no serious complaints to make; Mr. Henley will not be recognized, he will doubtless never even read what I have written, and even if he *should* read it, if he *should* recognize himself—what then?

---

[1] Certain references are omitted from this letter, to the novel by Samuel de Constant, which deals with the marital troubles of a husband, and which was well-known in Switzerland at that date and was even translated into English.

Let me begin.

Although left an orphan and almost penniless at a tender age, I was nevertheless bred up in luxury and with a tenderness that no maternal love could have surpassed. My aunt, Lady Ailesford, having lost her only daughter, adopted me in her stead, and the fondness and care which she lavished upon me led her in time to love me as if I had been her daughter indeed. Her husband had a nephew who was to inherit the property and the title; I was destined to be his bride. He was amiable, we were bred up in the notion that we were, one day, to be united. The idea was agreeable to us both; we loved each other without uneasiness. Then his uncle died. This change in his fortune effected no alteration in his heart; but he was sent abroad to travel. At Venice he merely diverted himself, but at Florence my image was effaced by more seductive charms. He passed some time at Naples, and, the following year, he died at Paris. I will not tell you all that I then suffered, all that for several months previously I had suffered. You, yourself, remarked at Montpellier the traces that sorrow had left on my temper and the hurt it had done to my health. My aunt was equally unhappy. Fifteen years of hope, fifteen years of care bestowed on a favourite project; all was useless, all was at an end. As for me I had lost all that a woman *has* to lose.

But at twenty years of age it is not possible to abandon all hope of consolation, and I returned

to England a trifle less unhappy than I had
left it.

My travels had formed and emboldened me; I
spoke French with greater ease; I sang better; I
was admired. I made conquests, but the envy of
other females was all the profit they procured me.
Inquisitive and critical observation pursued me in
the least of my actions, and feminine censure fixed
itself upon me. I did not love those who loved
me; I refused a rich man who was without birth
or breeding, I refused a man of rank who was
worn out and in debt; I refused a young man whose
adequacy in fortune was only comparable to his
stupidity. I was considered haughty; my old
friends quizzed me; society became odious to me.
My aunt, without blaming me, warned me repeat-
edly that the three thousand pounds which were
paid her annually ceased with her death, and that
she had not three thousand pounds of capital to
leave me.

Such was my situation, a year ago, when we
went to pass the Christmas holidays with Lady
Waltham. I was twenty-five years of age; my
heart was bruised and empty and I was beginning
to curse the tastes and the talents that had only
caused me to banish false hopes, an unhappy nice-
ness, and a pretension to felicity that had not been
realized.

There were two unmarried men in the house.
The one, forty years of age, had come from the
Indies with a considerable fortune. There were

no grave accusations to his charge as to the means by which he had acquired it, but neither was his reputation for scrupulous delicacy untarnished; and in the conversations which we had on the wealth and the wealthy of that country, he shunned particulars. He was a handsome man, free and noble in his manners and mode of life; he was partial to conversation, the fine arts, and the pleasures of the world. I proved attractive to him; he spoke to my aunt and offered in return for my hand a considerable dowry, the ownership of a fine mansion, which he had just purchased in London, and three hundred guineas a year as pin money.

The other marriageable man was the second son of the Earl of Reading. He was aged thirty-five, and had since the last four years been rendered a widower through the death of a wife who had bequeathed him a large fortune. He was the father of a little girl of five, of angelic beauty. He himself was of the noblest countenance, tall, with the slenderest figure, the softest blue eyes, the most beautiful teeth, the sweetest smile; such, my dear friend, was Mr. Henley, or such he appeared to me. I thought that all he said was in harmony with this agreeable exterior. He frequently spoke to me of the life which he led in the country and of the felicity that might be enjoyed there were his solitude shared with an amiable and intelligent companion, possessed of a good understanding and agreeable talents. He spoke to me of his daughter and of his desire to give her, not a governess, not a stepmother, but a mother. At last he spoke even more plainly, and on the eve of our departure, he made my aunt the most generous offers on my behalf. I felt, if not moved by passion, at least touched by emotion. On our return to London my aunt informed herself about my two admirers; she learned nothing disadvantageous about the first, but of the second she heard all that was most favourable. Reasonableness, learning, justice, and perfect evenness of temper, that is what every voice accorded to Mr. Henley. I saw that I must make my choice, and you can easily imagine, my dear friend, that I did not permit myself to hesitate. It was, so to speak, the baser part of my heart which preferred the riches of the East, the pleasures of the town, a greater liberty and a more splendid fortune; the nobler part despised all that and dwelt upon the felicity of a union that was to be all reason, all sweetness, and which the angels might applaud. If a tyrannous father had compelled me to marry the Nabob I should perhaps have made a duty of obeying him and should have endeavoured to forget the origin of my fortune in the use that I should have made of it. " The blessings of the poor of Europe will divert from me," I should have said, " the curses of India." In a word, had I been compelled to become happy in a vulgar fashion I should have become so without shame and even perhaps with pleasure; but to give myself by my own free will, in exchange for diamonds, pearls, carpets, perfumes, and worked muslins, for suppers and routs, that I could not prevail upon myself to do. I promised my hand to Mr. Henley.

Our wedding was charming. Witty, elegant, polite, considerate, and affectionate, Mr. Henley enchanted everyone; he was a husband of romance; be even seemed to me sometimes to be a little *too* perfect; my whims, my moods, and my impatience found his reasonableness and moderation always in their path. I felt, for instance, with regard to my presentation at Court, sorrows and joys which he did not appear to comprehend.

I persuaded myself that the society of a man I so much admired would cause me to resemble him, and I left for his country estate at the beginning of the Spring, full of good intentions, and convinced that I was going to be the best wife, the most tender stepmother, and the most worthy mistress of a house that had ever been seen. Sometimes I proposed myself as models the noblest Roman matrons, sometimes the wives of our ancient barons in feudal days; at other times I pictured myself rambling about the country as simple as a shepherdess, as gentle as her lambs, and as gay as the birds that I heard warbling.

But this, my dear friend, is a sufficiently long letter; I will take up my pen again at the first opportunity.

We arrived at Hollow Park. It is an ancient, handsome, and stately mansion that had been bequeathed to Mr. Henley by his mother, the heiress of the Astley family.

I delighted in everything. I was moved when I saw white-haired servants running to meet their beloved master and to bless their new mistress. They brought the child to me; what caresses did I not lavish upon her! In my heart I vowed to her the most assiduous care, the most tender attachment. I passed the remainder of that day in a kind of delirium; the next day I dressed up the child in the finery that I had brought her from London and led her to her father, expecting to cause him an agreeable surprise.

"Your intention is charming," he said, "but this is a taste that I should scarcely desire to arouse in her. I fear that such pretty shoes may prevent her running about freely; and artificial flowers contrast disagreeably with the simplicity of the country."

"You are in the right, sir," I replied, "I was in the wrong to dress her up in that manner, and now I do not know how to take all this finery from her; I wished to attach her to me by childish means, and I have only prepared a little disappointment for her, and, for myself, a mortification."

Fortunately the shoes were soon spoiled, the

locket lost, the flowers of the hat caught on the bushes and left there; and I took such pains to divert the child that she had not the time to regret her losses.

She was able to read in French as well as in English, and I began to teach her La Fontaine's fables. She recited to her father one day the fable of the oak and the reed with charming grace. I repeated the words in a whisper before her; my heart beat, I was flushed with pleasure. " She recites wonderfully," said Mr. Henley, " but does she understand what she recites ? It might perhaps be wiser to put into her head truths before fictions; history, geography——"

" You are perfectly right, sir," I said, " but her nurse could teach her just as well as I can that Paris is on the Seine and Lisbon on the Tagus."

" Why this impatience ? " continued Mr. Henley gently; " by all means teach her La Fontaine's fables if it pleases you; at bottom there is not much harm in it."

" No," I replied with vivacity; " she is not my child, she is yours."

" But, my dearest, I had hoped——"

I did not stay to answer him, but went away in tears. I was in the wrong, I know very well; it was I who was in the wrong. I returned a little later and Mr. Henley appeared not even to recollect my impatience. The child was fidgetting and yawning beside him, without his even observing her.

A few days afterwards I tried to establish a

history and geography lesson; it soon wearied both the mistress and the pupil. Her father considered her too young to learn music and questioned whether that species of talent did not produce more pretension than pleasure. The little girl, having nothing better to do when with me than to trifle tiresomely or to follow my movements with a gaze that was sometimes vacant and sometimes inquisitive, became troublesome to me, and I almost banished her from my room. She had grown unaccustomed to being with her nurse. The poor child is certainly less happy and less well-behaved than before I came here. But for my care of her during the smallpox, which she had just had, and which I myself took, through nursing her day and night, I should scarcely know that the little girl interested me more than the child of a stranger.

As to the servants no one has reason to complain of me, but my elegant waiting maid has dazzled a neighbouring farmer who was in love previously with the daughter of our old and excellent housekeeper, the foster sister of my husband's mother. The daughter, disconsolate, and the mother, outraged, by this affront, have left the house, in spite of all our remonstrances. I replace their loss as best I can, assisted by my maid, who is of a perfectly good character, or I should have dismissed her immediately. But the whole household misses the old housekeeper, and I, too, regret her and the excellent preserves that she used to make.

I had brought with me from London a superb white Angora cat. Mr. Henley did not think him handsomer than any other cat, and would often joke over the sway of fashion which decided the lot of animals, drawing down upon them exaggerated admiration or humiliating scorn, as upon our own gowns or head-dresses. He, however, petted the Angora, for he is kindly, and refuses to no creature endowed with sensibility some small token of his own.—But it is not exactly the story of my cat that I desire to tell you.—My room was upholstered in stripes; very dark green velvet separating pieces of embroidery, worked by Mr. Henley's grandmother. Large armchairs, vastly inconvenient to move but excellent for sleeping on, embroidered by the same hand and bordered by the same velvet, together with a monstrous hard sofa, completed the furnishings of my apartment. My Angora used to sleep disrespectfully upon the old armchairs and to become entangled in the antique needlework. Mr. Henley had already placed him gently on the ground several times. Six months ago, when he was dressed for hunting and had come to bid me good-bye in my room he saw the cat again asleep on an armchair.

" Ah! " he exclaimed, " what would my grandmother, what would my mother say if they saw this? "

" They would undoubtedly say," I replied with warmth, " that I ought to make use of my furniture in my own fashion as they made use of theirs,

and that I ought not to be a stranger even in my
own apartment; and from the time that I complained to you of these heavy armchairs and this
sad upholstery they would have prayed you to
give me other chairs and other hangings."

"*Give*, my dearest life!" answered Mr. Henley,
"does one then *give* to oneself? Does half of
oneself give to the other half? Are you not
mistress here? Formerly all this was thought very
fine——"

"Yes, *formerly*," I replied, "but I live *now*."

"My first wife," continued Mr. Henley, "liked
this furniture——"

"Ah, good God!" I exclaimed, "would that
she were still alive!"

"And all this for a cat to whom I have done no
harm!" said Mr. Henley, with a sad and gentle
look, a look of resignation; and he went away.

"No," I cried after him, "it is *not* the cat."
But he was already far away, and a moment later
I heard him tranquilly giving some orders in the
yard while he mounted his horse.

This composure put me quite beside myself. I
rang. (He had said that I was mistress here.) I
had the armchairs carried into the withdrawing
room, the sofa into a vestibule. I commanded a
lackey to take down the portrait of the first
Mistress Henley, which hung opposite my bed.
"But, Madam," he said. "Obey me or leave,"
I replied.

He doubtless believed, and so will you, that I

nourished a grudge against the portrait; but indeed I do not think this to have been the case. It was, however, hung upon the needlework, and, as I desired to remove that it was necessary to commence with the portrait. The embroidery came next; it was only hung upon hooks, I had it cleaned and carefully rolled. I had some basketwork chairs put in my room, and I, myself, arranged a cushion for my Angora; but the poor animal did not profit by my attentions; terrified by all this bustle he had fled into the park, and was never again seen.

Mr. Henley, when he returned from hunting, observed with surprise his wife's portrait in the dining parlour. He came up to my room without saying anything about it to me, and promptly wrote to London to order to be sent me the most beautiful Chinese paper, the most elegant chairs, and the finest worked muslin for hangings.

Was I in the wrong, my dear friend, except in my fashion of acting? Has what is old any more merit than that which is new? As for the folk who pass for reasonable do they not merely oppose with solemnity their prejudices and their tastes to other prejudices, other tastes expressed perhaps with more vivacity?

The question of the relatives is of greater importance. There are some whom I receive with my best grace, because their circumstances are not easy; but I yawn in their company, and never go to see them of my own accord, because they are

the most tedious folk alive. When Mr. Henley
says to me quite simply, " Let us go and see my
cousin so-and-so," I go; I am in the chariot or on
horseback with him, and that cannot be disagreeable to me. But if he comes and says to me, " My
cousin is a good woman," I reply, " No; she is
fault-finding, jealous, and tetchy." If he says that
a certain gentleman who is his cousin is an honest
man whom he esteems, I reply that he is a coarse
drunkard. I speak the truth but I am in the wrong,
for I cause my husband pain.

I am on excellent terms with my father-in-law;
he has middling parts and great good humour.
I embroider him waistcoats and play him the
harpsichord. But Lady Sara Melville, my sister-
in-law, who lives with him all the summer, is so
condescending to me that it renders the place
intolerable, and I but seldom go there. If Mr.
Henley were to say to me, " Endure these airs
for love of me; I will love you all the better; I
feel them for you as for myself; but I love my
father and my brother; your coldness will gradually separate them from me, and you, yourself,
will be chagrined by the diminution of happiness
and of sweet and natural sentiments that you have
occasioned." I should then undoubtedly say,
" You are in the right, Mr. Henley; I already feel,
I have indeed often felt, the regret that you
suggest; it will increase, it distresses me more than
I can say; let us go to my lord, an affectionate
glance from you will give me more pleasure than

all the pain that Lady Sara's ridiculous scorn can afford me."

But instead of that Mr. Henley has observed nothing, can recollect nothing. " Now that you mention it, my dear, I believe I do dimly remember. . . . But, even if it were so, what does it signify? How can a reasonable woman mind? And, besides, is not Lady Sara excusable? A duke's daughter, and the wife of the future head of our family. . . ."

My dear friend, blows would vex me less than all this reasonableness. I am unhappy, I am dull; I have not brought happiness to this house and neither have I found it; I have been the cause of unsettlement, but am not myself settled; I regret my errors but I have been afforded no means of avoiding them. I am alone; no one feels with me; and I am all the more unhappy because there is nothing of which I can complain, no alteration which I can ask, no reproach which I can make, so that I blame and despise myself for my own unhappiness. Everyone admires Mr. Henley and compliments me on my happiness, and I reply, " It is true, you are perfectly in the right. . . . What a contrast does he not present with other men of his age and rank? What a contrast between my lot and that of madam this or my lady that."

I say it, I think it, and my heart does not feel it; it swells or contracts and I withdraw in order to weep at my ease. Even at this moment, tears of which I scarcely comprehend the origin, are blended with the ink of this letter. Farewell, my dear friend, I shall not delay in writing to you further.

P.S.—On re-reading my letter I find that I have been more in the wrong than I believed. I will have the first Mistress Henley's portrait put back in its old place. If Mr. Henley considers that it looks better in the dining parlour, where it hangs indeed in a better light, he has only to have it taken back; I shall summon the same lackey who removed it from my apartment. When he has replaced the portrait I will bid him have the horses put to the chariot and I shall go to visit my father-in-law.

LETTER III

You are quite right, my love, and it was not for me to complain of the injustice which might be occasioned by the *Sentimental Husband*.[1] Yet I spoke in good faith, and, even to-day, my ideas on this subject are not very precise. Whether through patience or indifference, through merit or disposition, it does not appear to me that Mr. Henley has been unhappy. He has remarked, I do not doubt, each of our errors. But he has expressed no resentment nor has he sought by a more intimate association of my mind and my pleasures with his own to prevent further errors on my part. I have therefore

[1] The novel referred to in the first letter.

47

reason to believe that he has drawn no conclusions from the whole business. He has lived, he has judged me, from day to day, until the author of this Swiss romance contrived to make him conscious of his satisfaction with himself, and of his dissatisfaction with me.

I have suffered many vexations since my last letter. One day, when I was lamenting the smallness of my capacity for household affairs, the slowness of my progress, and the variableness of my zeal and my efforts, Mr. Henley proceeded, although quite pleasantly, and with a smile, to enumerate all the matters which had gone less smoothly since the departure of Mrs. Grace.

"Let us endeavour to procure her return," I immediately replied, "I have heard that Peggy is established in London and that her mother is but middlingly comfortable with the cousin with whom she has taken up her abode."

"You can but try," said Mr. Henley. "I fear that you will not succeed, but there can be no hurt in trying."

"Will *you* not speak to her?" I asked; "the sight of her old master thus eager for her return would assuredly cause her to forget all her resentment."

"It is not in my power," he answered, "I have business; but, if you desire it, I will send——"

"No; I will go myself."

I ordered the chariot and went. It was four miles away, Mrs. Grace was alone and was vastly

surprised to see me. Through all the coldness
which she endeavoured to put into her compliments I could perceive her emotion, together with
a confusion of spirits of which I could not divine
the cause. I told her how much we had suffered
through her departure, how much we missed her,
how much she was regretted.

"Will you not return?" I asked. "You will
find yourself esteemed and beloved. Why should
you blame us all on account of the inconstancy of
a young man who does not even deserve Peggy's
regrets, since he has abandoned her? Maybe she
herself has forgotten him.—I have learned that
she is established in London——"

"Established!" exclaimed Mrs. Grace, clasping
her hands and lifting her eyes to heaven; "do you
come here, madam, to affront me?"

"God forbid!" I cried in my turn. "I do not
take your meaning."

"Ah, madam," she continued after a prolonged
silence; "evils are not remedied so quickly as they
are caused, and your Fanny, with her laces, her
ribbons, and her town airs has brought upon my
Peggy and her poor mother sorrows that will end
only with our lives."

And she wept bitterly. Constrained by my
caresses and entreaties, she narrated to me, between
her sobs, the story of her troubles. Peggy, distressed by the loss of her lover and dull in the
company of her mother and her cousin, departed
without a word. They sought long for her, and

for a time it was believed that she had drowned
herself, but eventually it was discovered that she
was in London, where her youth and her freshness
had caused her to be received in a house of ill
fame. You can easily imagine all that her mother
added to this sad story, all that I said, all that I felt.
Finally I repeated my first proposition. Despite a
thousand natural and just objections, of which I
admitted the full force, I yet was able to persuade
the poor soul to return with me to Hollow Park.

"No one," I said to her, "will speak to you of
your daughter; you need not see Fanny until you
tell me that you desire to see her. Come, my good
Mrs. Grace, come and seek some consolation and
end your days in a house in which you rendered
such good service in your youth and which you
should never have been permitted to leave."

I placed her in the chariot, not wishing to give
her time while she made up her packages for
further reflections that might hinder her coming.
On the road she never ceased weeping; and I
wept in sympathy. When a hundred yards distant
from the house I descended from the chariot and
bade the coachman proceed no further until he
had received my order to do so. I entered the
house alone; I spoke to Mr. Henley, to the child,
to Fanny, and to the other servants. Then I went
to fetch Mrs. Grace and, giving over to her my
keys, I prayed her to take up her charge at once.

Five or six days passed; Fanny obeyed me
scrupulously, eating and working in her own

chamber. One day, when I had gone there to look at her work, Mrs. Grace came with me, and, after having thanked me for my kindness, she prayed me to agree to Fanny's dining with the other domestics and living in the house as before. Fanny was overcome, and wept for the unhappy Peggy and her mother. Poor Fanny! her turn was yet to come. Mr. Henley shortly afterwards desired me to step downstairs and to bring her with me. We found with him in his cabinet the father of the young farmer, Fanny's admirer.

"Madam," he said, "I have come to beg Mr. Henley and yourself to give my son letters of recommendation for the Indies. It is a country where, they say, men speedily grow rich; he can carry Miss with him there or come back to marry her when he has become a rich gentleman. They can do as they please; but I will never receive in my house an idle and coquettish city doll; besides, I should think to be drawing down the curses of heaven upon myself, by permitting the entrance into my family of one who by her cursed arts has been the cause of my son's inconstancy and poor Peggy's ruin. My son will do as he pleases, miss; but I declare before God that he will lose both his father and his roof if he ever sees you again."

Fanny, pale as death, attempted to quit the room; but her limbs trembled beneath her and she leaned against the door. I ran immediately to her aid and helped her back to her room. We met Mrs. Grace on the stair; "Your daughter is avenged," Fanny said to her. "Lord! what has happened?" cried Mrs. Grace. She followed us; I told her what had passed, and she swore to us that she had had no part in these proceedings and had not even seen the farmer or his son since her departure from the house. I left them; and went to shut myself up in my own apartment, bitterly lamenting the fate of both the girls, and all the mischief of which I had been the cause. Then I wrote to my aunt that I was sending Fanny back to her, and implored her to find her a good place either with a lady or with a milliner; having despatched an order to the coachman to harness as quickly as possible I returned to Fanny and made her read my letter. The poor girl burst into tears.

"But what have I done?" she cried. "Nothing, my dear child, nothing that is wrong, but it is absolutely needful that we should part. I shall pay your wages until the end of the year and shall add more money and clothes than as yet you can desire to receive from a mistress whom you must certainly consider unjust. I shall write to your parents to send me your younger sister; but you must come with me at once, and I will take you to the place where the London coach will pass an hour hence. Mrs. Grace and I will take charge of all that you leave here and you will receive your possessions in two days." The chariot was soon ready. I entered it with her, and we arrived, almost without exchanging a word, at the place that I had named. I awaited the coach; I recommended Fanny to the kindness of the passengers, and I returned more dejected than it is possible to say. " So *that*," I said to myself, " is what I have done here. I have occasioned the ruin of one poor and innocent girl, I have made another unhappy, I have caused a father to quarrel with his son, and I have filled a mother's heart with shame and bitterness! "

In passing through the park I wept for my Angora, and on entering my room I wept for Fanny. Mrs. Grace has since then served me as waiting maid. Her sadness, which however she endeavours to master, is a perpetual reproach. Mr. Henley appears to be surprised by all this agitation. He does not quite understand why I dismissed my maid so suddenly. He thought the farmer quite in the right in opposing his son's marriage. " These women," he said, " accustomed to the town, never take root in the country, and are good for nothing there." But he considered that the son might have been persuaded to listen to reason and that I might have kept Fanny; indeed, that they might have become detached from each other in continuing to see each other, while now the young man's imagination would prolong the illusion of love and he would perhaps make a point of honour of remaining true to his persecuted mistress.

That will happen which is God's will, but I have done what I believed to be right and have spared myself scenes which would certainly have affected my health and completed the change in my temper. It is fifteen days since Fanny left. My Lady C—— will keep her until she is able to place her. Her sister arrives this evening. She has only been in London sufficient time to learn to dress hair and has since then passed almost a year in her village. She is not pretty, and I shall do all that lies with me to prevent her from becoming elegant. Farewell, my dearest friend. . . .

P.S.—My letter could not leave the other day: the servant seeing me about to seal it warned me that it was too late for the mail.

Fanny's sister is dirty, clumsy, lazy, and impertinent; it will not be possible for me to keep her. Mr. Henley never ceases telling me that I did wrong to dismiss a girl whom I liked, who served me well, and who could be reproached for no fault. I should not have taken literally, he said, that which excitement made John Turner say; and he instanced as proof his mad notion of sending to the Indies a boy who does not even know how to write. He is surprised that we hasty folk should be the dupes of each other's exaggerations and extravagances. We should know, he opines, how great an allowance should be made for that which emotion makes us say and do. I have mistaken, he says, an action which cost me some sacrifice for one that was noble in itself, without reflecting that that which was disadvantageous to me might not necessarily be of advantage to others. It would have been more prudent never to have brought the girl here. He thought to have suggested this to me at the time, but since she *was* here, since she was not to blame, I should have kept her. . . . Was he in the right, my dear? Was I again in the wrong, always in the wrong, in the wrong in everything? No; I will not credit it; it was natural for me to keep Fanny when I married, and I did not understand Mr. Henley's warning. I did not know that it was difficult to accustom oneself to living in the country; was I not going to live there myself? Fanny might prove attractive to some rustic neighbour; might she not then marry him?—she was sweet and amiable. I had no notion that it would be a grief to his family and a misfortune to him. I did no wrong in sending her away, for I was not bound to make myself either her jailer or her accomplice, either by forbidding the young man's visits or by favouring them. I was not bound to take upon myself either their sorrows or their errors. With the passage of time, if she should forget her lover or he marry or go away, I might take her back; it is not my intention ever to forsake her.

I do, however, think myself to have been too precipitate. I might have waited a day or two, in order to consult Mr. Henley, to consult Fanny herself, and to see what could be hoped from her resolution and from the young man's filial obedience. I paid too much heed to the impetuosity of my own disposition. I was too apprehensive of the sight of unhappy passion and humiliated pride. May God keep Fanny from misfortune and me from remorse!

I will write again to my aunt, and once more recommend Fanny to her benevolence.

LETTER IV

I discourse to you, my dear friend, on very dull topics, and with what ¦prolixity, what detail! But it is thus that things appear to me, and I should feel myself to be telling you nothing if I did not tell you everything. They are trifles which distress or provoke me, and which put me in the wrong. Listen, therefore, once more to a tale of trifles.

Three weeks ago a ball was given at Guildford. Mr. Henley was one of the subscribers. A relative of Mr. Henley, who owns a house there, invited us to go to her the previous day and to carry the child with us. We went; I wore the costume which I desired to wear, a dress which I had worn at a London ball eighteen months ago, and a hat, feathers, and flowers which my aunt and Fanny had selected expressly for this entertainment and which I had received two days before. I had only myself seen them at the moment of putting them on, not having until then unpacked the bandbox. I was excessively pleased; I believed myself to look vastly fine when I was dressed, and I put on some red, as almost everyone does.

An hour before the ball Mr. Henley arrived from Hollow Park.

"You look very well, madam," he said, "for you cannot look otherwise; but I like you a hundred times better in your simplest clothes than in all this finery. It also appears to me that a woman of twenty-six should not be dressed like a girl of fifteen, or a respectable woman like an actress——"

Tears sprang to my eyes.

"Lady Ailesford," I replied, "in sending me this costume did not think herself to be dressing a girl of fifteen or an actress, but her niece and your wife, whose age she knew. . . . But, sir, you have only to say that this costume vexes or displeases you and I should give you pleasure in not appearing dressed in this manner, and I shall at once give up the ball, and, I hope, with a good grace."

"Could you not," he said, "send a man on horseback to fetch another dress, another hat?"

"No!" I said, "that is not possible. My woman is here, they would find nothing; I have nothing suitable; I should certainly disarrange my hair——"

"And what would that matter?" said Mr. Henley, smiling.

"It would matter to *me*," I exclaimed with warmth, "but if you prefer that I should not go to

57

the ball you have only to say so and I should be most happy to oblige you." And, half with vexation, half with sensibility, I began to weep in good earnest.

"I regret, madam," said Mr. Henley, "that this has touched you so closely. I shall not hinder you from going to the ball. You have not as yet I think found in me a very absolute husband. I should wish reason and prudence to prevail with you and not that you should yield to my prejudices; since your aunt has judged this costume suitable you had best remain as you are. . . . But you must replace the red which your tears have disarranged."

I smiled and kissed his hand in a transport of joy. "I perceive with pleasure," he said, "that my dear wife is as youthful as her head-dress and as light as her feathers."

I went to put back the red. Some of the company arrived, and, the hour for the ball having come, we started. In the carriage, I affected high spirits, in order to give them to Mr. Henley and myself. In this I was not successful. I did not know whether I had done right or wrong. I was dissatisfied with myself and ill at ease. We had been in the ballroom for a quarter of an hour when we perceived all eyes turned towards the door, attracted by the most noble of countenances and the simplest, most elegant and splendid of costumes. There was a whispering and a questioning, and everyone said "It is Lady Bridgewater, wife

of Governor Bridgewater, who has returned from
the Indies and has been made a baronet."

You must forgive my weakness; that moment
was not agreeable to me. Fortunately, another
object for comparison presented itself; my sister-
in-law entered, plastered with red; her feathers,
too, were a very different affair from mine.

" Look! " I said to Mr. Henley.

" She is not my wife," he replied.

And he went to take her hand to lead her to a
chair. " Other men," I thought, " will have a like
indulgence for me." A feeling of coquetry took
possession of my heart and I shook off my chagrin
in order to appear the more amiable during the
remainder of the evening. I had a reason for not
dancing which I do not as yet desire to reveal to
you.

After the first country dance Lady Bridgewater
came and seated herself beside me.

" I asked who you were, madam," she said with
the utmost sweetness of address; " and your name
alone has made of me an acquaintance, almost a
friend. There would be too much self-love in my
telling you how much this preference has been
assisted by your countenance; since my husband,
Sir John Bridgewater, who has frequently spoken
of you to me, has said that I greatly resemble you."

So much gentleness and candour quite won my
heart; my jealousy ought to have increased, but
in fact I ceased to feel it; for it gave place to a
sweet sensation of sympathy. It is indeed possible

that Lady Bridgewater resembles me; but she is younger than I am, taller, and with a more slender figure; her hair is finer; in short, she has the advantage of me in all those things about which one cannot cherish illusions, and, as to the others, I cannot even in those have the advantage of her, for it would not be possible to have a better grace or a tone of voice that goes more swiftly to the heart.

Mr. Henley was excessively assiduous in his attentions to Miss Clairville, a young girl of this county, who is uncommonly fresh and gay, but also extremely modest and not at all pretty. For my part I conversed during the whole evening with Lady Bridgewater and her brother, Mr. Mead, whom she presented to me; and I was, on the whole, well pleased with them and with myself.

I pressed them to visit me. Lady Bridgewater expressed great regret at being obliged to leave the country the following day, in order to return to London and then to rejoin her husband in Yorkshire, where he was contesting an election. As to Mr. Mead he accepted my invitation for the next day but one. We separated as late as possible.

I rested some hours at the house of Mr. Henley's cousin, and after breakfast we took our seats in the chariot, my husband, his daughter, and I. The nurse and my maid had already left. My mind was busy with Lady Bridgewater, and I thought to see again in my fancy her pleasing countenance and to hear once more her language and her tones.

" You must allow that she is charming," I said to Mr. Henley.

" Who is charming? " he replied.

" Is it possible," I said, " that you do not know."

" Ah! it seems that you are speaking of Lady Bridgewater. Yes; she is very well, she is a fine woman; and I thought her to be dressed with great elegance. I cannot say that she made a great impression upon me."

" Oh well! " I continued, " if little blue eyes, red hair, and a rustic air are points of beauty, Miss Clairville has undoubtedly the advantage of Lady Bridgewater and of all other women of her sort. For my part, the most agreeable person whom I saw at the ball, after Lady Bridgewater, was her brother; he put me in mind of my Lord Ailesford, my first *beau*; and I invited him to dine with us to-morrow."

" It is fortunate that I am not jealous," said Mr. Henley, smiling.

" Fortunate perhaps for *you*," I continued, " but not for me; for if you *were* jealous I should at least know that you felt something. I should think myself flattered; I should believe myself to be of value to you; I should believe that you feared to lose me, that I still pleased you, or, at the least, that you still thought me capable of pleasing. Yes; " I added, heated both by my own vivacity and by his imperturbable calm, " the injustice of a jealous man or the passion of a brutal one would be less vexatious to me than the phlegm and dryness of a sage."

"You would almost cause me to believe," said Mr. Henley, "in the taste of those Russian women who desire to be beaten. But, my dear, give over your warmth, for the sake of this child, and let us not set her a bad example."

"You are right," I exclaimed. "Forgive me, sir, forgive me, my child!" And lifting her on to my knee I embraced her, moistening her face with my tears.

"I am setting you a bad example," I said, "I should be taking your mother's place, as I promised you, instead of which I have no care of you and say before you things which you are happy in not wholly comprehending." Mr. Henley said nothing, but I saw that he was touched. The little girl remained on my knee and gave me some caresses which I returned to her a hundredfold, but with a sentiment that was even more regretful than it was tender. I felt bitterly repentant and was forming all kinds of projects, saying to myself that I would at last really become her mother. But I beheld in her eyes, that is to say in her soul, the impossibility of doing so. She is pretty, she is not vicious, she is not silly, but neither is she very lively or highly sensitive. She will be my *pupil* but she will not be and will not ever desire to be my *child*.

We arrived. At my request the company from Henley Hall was invited for the following day.

Miss Clairville was staying there, so she also came. At table I placed Mr. Mead between her and Lady Sara Melville, and nothing occurred during the day that was either provoking or remarkable. The next day I wrote a letter to Mr. Henley, of which I am sending you the rough copy, with all its erasures. There are almost as many words crossed out as left, and you will hardly read it without difficulty.

" SIR,
    " You observed, I trust, yesterday, how much I was ashamed of my excessive warmth. Do not think, on this occasion as on many others, the merit of your patience and your gentleness to have escaped me. I can assure you that my intentions have always been good. But of what use are intentions if they are never realized?
    " As to you, your behaviour has been such that I can discover nothing to blame in it, however much I may sometimes have desired to do so, in order to justify my own. You have, however, been guilty of one error; you did me too much honour in marrying me. You believed—and who would not have believed—that a rational woman, finding in her husband all that renders a man pleasing and respectable, and in her situation every honourable enjoyment, wealth, and consequence, would not fail to find also happiness. But I am not a rational woman, and we have both discovered it too late. I do not unite those qualities which would have

made us happy with those that appeared to you pleasing. You might have found both in a dozen other women.

"You did not ask for brilliant parts, since you were satisfied with me, and assuredly there is no one who makes less call on rare virtues. I only spoke of Miss Clairville with bitterness because I felt with chagrin how much better than I such a girl would have suited you. Accuſtomed to the pleasures and occupations of the country, active, induſtrious, simple in her taſtes, grateful, gay, and contented, she would never have tempted you to recollect those qualities in which she might be lacking. Miss Clairville would have remained here in the midſt of her family and her own mode of life. She would have loſt nothing; she would only have gained. . . . But it is idle to dwell upon a dream. The paſt cannot be recalled. Let us speak of the future, and, above all, of your daughter. Let us try to plan my conduct so as to repair the graveſt of my faults. In opposing at the beginning that which I tried to do for her, you said nothing that was not fair and reasonable; but you appeared to condemn all that had been done for me, and to scorn all that I knew and that I was. I was humiliated and discouraged; I proved lacking in pliancy and true goodwill. For the future I intend to do my duty, not according to my own ideas, but according to your judgment. I shall not ask you to make out a scheme for me; I shall endeavour to divine your views in order to

submit myself to them.   But if I divine ill or act
amiss, have the kindness, I beg you, not to blame
me merely, but to tell me what you would desire
me to do in place of what I am doing.   Upon this
point and upon all others I sincerely desire to
deserve your approbation, to gain or to regain
your affection, and to diminish in your heart your
regret over your unhappy choice.

" S. HENLEY."

I carried my letter to Mr. Henley in his cabinet,
and withdrew.   A quarter of an hour later he came
to join me in the parlour.

" Have I made any complaints, madam? " he
said, embracing me.   " Have I spoken of Miss
Clairville?   Have I thought of any Miss Clairville? "

At that moment his father and brother entering,
I hid my emotion.   It appeared to me that during
their visit Mr. Henley was more assiduous and
looked at me with greater frequency than was his
custom; it was the best reply that he could have
made.   We never spoke of the matter again.

Since that day I rise earlier, and have Miss
Henley to breakfast with me.   She takes a writing
lesson in my room and I give her one in geography,
in some rudiments of history, and some principles
of religion.

I will not speak of my success with the child.
There I must wait and hope.   Neither will I speak
of all my efforts to render the country more inter-

esting to myself. This place resembles its master; it is too perfect; there is nothing for me to change, nothing which calls for my exertion or my care. An ancient lime tree screens from my windows a sufficiently fine prospect; I wished it to be cut down; but when I looked at it more closely I myself felt that to do so would be a sad pity. That which affords me the greatest pleasure in the vernal season is to watch the leaves appearing and unfolding, the flowers expanding, and a crowd of insects creeping, flying, scurrying hither and thither amid the boughs of this tree. I know nothing about these things, I attempt to learn nothing, but I contemplate and admire a universe that is so crowded and so animated. I lose myself in an immensity that is so prodigious (I cannot say so wise, for I am too ignorant). I do not know its purpose, its end, or its means; I do not even know why a voracious spider should be given so many little flies to devour; but I look, and the hours pass without my thinking either about myself or about my puerile discomfitures.

LETTER V

I can no longer doubt, my dearest friend, that I am with child; I have just now written to inform my aunt and to beg her to communicate the fact to Mr. Henley, who has been in London for some days past. I am overjoyed, and I intend to redouble my care of Miss Henley. For more than a year I was nothing to her, during the last two months I have been a tolerable mother; I must not now become a stepmother. *Adieu.* You will hear no more from me to-day.

I am far from well, my dear friend. I cannot relate to you all at one time what I desire to say. The task will be long and far from agreeable. I shall rest whenever I am fatigued. It is of little consequence whether you receive this letter some weeks sooner or later. After it I shall write no more of the sort; a note will inform you at infrequent intervals that your friend still lives, until her life is ended. Either my situation is in truth unhappy or I am a being devoid of virtue and sense. Confronted with this vexatious alternative, either of accusing fate, which I cannot change, or of accusing and despising myself, wheresoever I turn I find in the pictures which present themselves to my imagination and the incidents with which my memory is stored, matter to depress my courage and to render my existence gloomy and painful. To what purpose should I bring to life again through my narrative impressions in themselves distressing, or retrace scenes

67

which cannot be too soon or too completely forgotten?   Once again and for this last time you
will see into my heart; henceforth I shall forbid
myself complaint; I must either change my character or unbosom myself no more.   When I
thought myself assured of my condition, I had
Mr. Henley informed of it by my aunt.   He only
returned from London eight days later.   Through-
out that interval I never ceased to question myself
as to whether I ought, and whether I desired, to
nurse my child.   On the one side I was alarmed by
the fatigue, the continual care, the privations
which I should be obliged to impose upon myself.
And, dare I confess it? I was also afraid of the
injury that nursing inflicts on the female form.
Yet, on the other hand, I feared, as a great humiliation, to be accounted incapable or unworthy of
fulfilling this natural duty.   But, you will ask, was
it *only* a question of pride?   Did you not conceive
a great happiness in being everything to your
child, in attaching him to you, in attaching yourself to him, by every possible bond?   Yes, undoubtedly; and that was my most constant idea;
but when one is alone and always thinking of the
same thing, what varied thoughts do not pass
through the mind?

I resolved to speak of the matter to Mr. Henley;
and it was not without difficulty that I opened the
conversation.   I was in almost equal apprehension
of his approving my plan as a matter of course,
about which I was in the wrong to hesitate, or of

his rejecting it as an absurdity because of reasons which would cause me humiliation.

I was spared neither of these chagrins. According to his opinion nothing in the world could exempt a mother from the first and most sacred of her duties save the danger of injuring her infant through some fault in her own temper or character; and he informed me that it was his intention to consult his friend Dr. M—— in order to learn whether my prodigious liveliness and my frequent impatience might not make a stranger preferable for the task. Of myself, my health, or my happiness, not a word; the only consideration was the child, who did not as yet exist. This time I did not dispute or fly into a passion, I was only afflicted, but so profoundly afflicted that my health was affected. "Good God!" I thought, "so none of my sensations are divined, none of my sentiments shared! no suffering is to be spared me! Either all that I am feeling is absurd or Mr. Henley is totally lacking in sensibility. I must pass my whole life with a husband to whom I inspire only indifference, and whose heart is closed to me. Farewell to felicity in my pregnancy, farewell to all felicity!" And I fell into utter dejection.

Mrs. Grace was the first to observe this and spoke of it to Mr. Henley, who did not conceive the cause. He thought that my condition was occasioning my dejection and suggested that I should press my aunt to visit me. I welcomed this idea with gratitude; we wrote to my aunt,

and she came to us. To-morrow, if I am able, I
shall again take up my pen. . . .

*　　*　　*　　*　　*

I told nothing of all this to my aunt, and I
rather sought for distractions from her conversation than consolation from her tenderness. Sensibility plunged me back into sorrow; in order to
escape it I was compelled to escape from myself,
to distract and to forget myself and my situation.

The intrigues of the Court, the news of the
town, love affairs, marriages, appointments, all the
vanities and frivolities of the fashionable world,
restored to me my natural gaiety; a perilous gift,
of which the benefit was but passing and which was
to bring fresh sorrows upon me.

Very soon I only thought of my son or my
daughter as of a prodigy of beauty, whose brilliant
talents, cultivated by the most marvellous education, would excite the admiration of the whole
country, nay of the whole world. My daughter,
even handsomer than Lady Bridgewater, would
choose a husband from the noblest in the land;
my son, if he took up the profession of arms, would
become a hero and command armies, or, if he gave
himself to the law, would be at the least Lord
Mansfield or the Lord Chancellor, and a permanent
chancellor at that, whom his King and country
could never spare. . . . By dint of stuffing my head
with these extravagances, I grew incapable of
hiding them completely from Mr. Henley. I

laughed, however, myself, at my own folly, for I was not entirely lunatick. One day, half in jest, half in earnest (or at least thinking myself to be in earnest), I unfolded my dreams. . . . But I am becoming so agitated at the recollection that I must lay down my pen. . . .

* * * * *

We were alone; and Mr. Henley replied to me: "Our notions are very different; I desire my daughters to be bred up with simplicity, that they may attract but little attention and think but little of attracting it; that they may be modest, gentle, and rational, complaisant as wives and circumspect as mothers; that they may know how to enjoy riches, but that, above all, they may be able to dispense with it; I should wish their situation to be more apt to assure them virtues than to afford them renown; and, if all cannot be united, he said in kissing my hand, "I should content myself with but half of the grace, the talents, and the politeness of Mistress Henley. As to my son, a robust body, a healthy mind—that is to say, one free from vice or weakness—the strictest probity, which demands always the extremest moderation, that is what I would ask of God for him. But, my dearest," he continued, "since you attach so much importance to all that is brilliant, I would not have you run the risk of learning from others something which occurred a few days back. At the first moment you might be too much affected, and show to the

world by hasty expression of chagrin that husband
and wife had not but one soul between them, nor
but one single mode of thought and feeling. I was
offered a seat in Parliament and a place at court; I
was permitted to hope for a title for myself and
an appointment for you; I refused it all."

"Nothing would appear more natural to me,
sir," I replied, resting my face on my hands, for
fear that my emotion should betray itself, and
speaking slowly, in a voice of enforced composure—"nothing would appear to be more
natural, if the Government desired to purchase
with these offers a vote contrary to your principles;
but you approve the measures of the present
ministry?"

"Yes," he answered, "I am attached to the
King and I approve what the ministers are doing
to-day. But am I sure of approving what they
will do to-morrow? Is it certain that these
ministers will remain in office? And ought I to
risk the danger of feeling myself deprived by a
cabal of an office which has in truth no connection
with politics? Driven back to this place, which
has always been agreeable to me, should I not risk
finding it changed and spoiled, because I should
myself be changed, and because I should carry
back with me wounded self-love, frustrated
ambition, and passions to which, until now, I had
been a stranger?"

"I admire you, sir," I said. And, in truth, I had
never so much admired him; the more it cost me

the more I admired him; never had I perceived so clearly his superiority. "I admire you; nevertheless, the public good, the duty of serving one's country——"

"These are the pretexts of the ambitious," he interrupted. "The good that a man can do in his own house, amongst his neighbours, his friends, and his relatives is much more certain and more indispensable; and if I do not do all that I ought to do it is my own fault, and not that of my situation. I have lived far too long in London and in the large towns of the Continent, and so have lost sight of the occupations and interests of the country folk. I have not the gift of conversing and instructing myself among them, nor the activity that I should desire to possess. I should carry these defects to public places and I should be the more to blame since I had put myself *there*, while it was Providence that put me *here*."

"I have nothing more to say, sir," I said; "but why did you keep all this secret from me?"

"I was in London," he replied, "and it would have been difficult to me to detail you my reasons in a letter. If you had opposed your arguments and your tastes you would not have shaken me, and I should have had the grief of causing you chagrin that I might have spared you. Even to-day I was pained to have been compelled to speak of it, and if I had not learned that the matter had become in a manner public, you would never have heard either of the offer or of its refusal."

73

Mr. Henley had ceased speaking for at least a minute. I desired to say something; but I had been so attentive, I was so much torn between the esteem that such moderation, sense, and uprightness in my husband extorted from me, and the horror of seeing myself so foreign to his sentiments, so completely shut out from his thoughts, so useless, so isolated, that I could not utter. Exhausted by so much effort my head grew confused and I fainted. The care that was had of me hindered the consequences that this accident might have occasioned; but I am nevertheless not yet completely recovered. Neither my mind nor my body are in a natural condition. I am only a woman, and I shall not take my own life, I should not have the courage; and, if I become a mother, I hope never to have the desire; but sorrow itself can prove fatal. In a year, in two years, you will learn, I trust, that I am rational and contented, or that I am no more. . . .

LETTERS FROM LAUSANNE

LETTERS FROM LAUSANNE

(From Madam de C. to a friend in Languedoc)
30th November 1784.

HOW FOOLISH YOU ARE TO COMPLAIN! A SON-
in-law of middling parts, whom your
daughter has married without reluctance;
an establishment which you, yourself, approve, but
upon which you were hardly consulted! What
harm is there in all that? Why do you object?
Your husband, his parents, and considerations of
fortune decided it all. So much the better! If
your daughter is happy will you be therefore less
sensible of her felicity? If she is unhappy will it
not be one sorrow the less not to have decided her
fate? How romantic you are! Your son-in-law
is commonplace; but has your daughter then so
superior a character and intelligence? She is
indeed separated from you; but had you so much
pleasure in having her with you? She will live in
Paris; has she any disinclination to living there?
In spite of your protests against the dangers of the
capital, its seduction, illusion, prestige, excitement, and so forth, would you have any disinclination to living there yourself? You are still
handsome, you will always be amiable; I am much
mistaken if you would not yourself be willing to
load yourself with " the chains of the court," were
they to be offered to you. I think they *will* be

77

offered to you. At the time of her marriage you
will be spoken of, and it will be felt what an
advantage it would be to the princess who could
attach to her service a woman of your merit, discreet without prudery, equally sincere and polite,
modest, although full of talent. I wonder though
if that be indeed the case! I have always thought
that such diversity of merits only existed on paper,
where words never dispute, whatever contradic-
tions they may hold. Discreet and not prudish!
It is certain that you are not prudish: I have
always *seen* you very discreet; but have I always
seen you? Have you narrated to me the history of
every moment of your life? A perfectly discreet
woman must be a prude; at least I think so.
However, we will not dwell on that. Sincere and
polite! You are not as sincere as it would be
possible to be, since you are polite; nor perfectly
polite, since you are sincere; and you are only both
simultaneously because you are but middlingly
either. But enough! It is not you whom I am
blaming; I had need only of a vent to my feelings.
My daughter's guardians plague me about her
education; they tell me and write to me that a
young girl should acquire the accomplishments
which please the world, without caring to please.
And where, in heaven's name, is she to find
patience and perseverance for her harpsichord
lessons if she is indifferent to pleasing? They
desire her to be both frank and reserved. What is
the meaning of that? They wish her to fear

censure without desiring praise.   They applaud all
my tenderness for her; but would like me to be
less constantly occupied in preventing pain and
procuring pleasure for her.   That is how, with a
juxtaposition of words, people create impossible
characters, laws, educations, and domestic felicities.
With ideas like these they plague women, mothers,
young girls, and all the imbeciles who allow themselves to be preached to.   Let us return to you,
who are as sincere and as polite as it is necessary
to be; to you, whom I love tenderly.   The
Marquis of X—— said to me the other day that
he was almost sure that they would drag you out
from the country.   Very well!   Let yourself be
placed at Court, without complaining of what your
family demands of you.   Let yourself be ruled by
circumstances, and think yourself fortunate that
there *are* circumstances to rule you, relatives to
insist, a father to make a marriage for his daughter,
a daughter not too full of sensibility and reason to
permit herself to be married.   If only I were in
your place!   How much, as I observe your lot,
I am tempted to blame the religious zeal of my
grandfather!   If, like his brother, he had consented
to go to mass, I do not know if he would have
found himself as well off in another world; but it
seems to me that I should have found myself far
better off in this one.   Now indeed I often pity
myself; and think myself truly pitiable.   My poor
Cecilia, what will happen to her?   She was seventeen last spring.   It was necessary to take her into

society, in order to show society to her, and to
show her to young men who might perhaps think
of her. *Think* of her! What an absurd phrase!
Who is going to *think* of a girl whose mother is
still young, and who may, after the death of that
mother, have twenty-six thousand francs in this
country, that is to say, about thirty-eight thousand
francs in France! We possess, my daughter and I,
an income of fifteen hundred French francs. You
will therefore easily realize that if anyone marries
Cecilia, it will not be because he has *thought* of, but
because he has *seen* her. She must therefore be
shown off; she must also be amused, allowed to
dance. Yet she must not be shown off too much,
for fear people should tire of her; or amused too
much, for fear she should not be able to dispense
with amusement, for fear, too, that her guardians
should scold me, for fear that other mothers
should say: " How imprudent! She has so small
a fortune! What waste of time in dress, not to
speak of the time spent in society! " And then her
finery, modest as it is, does cost something;
muslins, ribbons, and all the rest; and nothing is
so petty, so precise, so detailed in such matters as
female censure. She must not be allowed to dance
too much; dancing heats and does not become her;
her hair, not too well dressed by herself and by
me, gives her, when tumbled, a rustic look; she
becomes too red and the next day has the headache
or a nose-bleeding; but she loves dancing passionately; she is pretty tall, well-proportioned, agile;

to hinder her from dancing would be like hindering a deer from running.

I have juſt told you what my daughter is like in her person; I will now describe her countenance. Imagine a pretty forehead, a pretty nose, black eyes somewhat deep-set, not vaſtly big but brilliant and soft; lips rather full and of a bright vermilion, good teeth, a fine dark skin and lively complexion, a throat which begins to grow thick despite all the pains that I take, a neck which would be beautiful if it were whiter, a passable foot and hand; that is my Cecilia. If you knew Madame R——, or any of the handsome peasant girls of the Pays-de-Vaud, I could give you a better idea of her. Would you like to know what charaĉter this appearance denotes? I will tell you; it means good health, good temper, gaiety, sensibility in matters of the heart and simplicity and uprightness in those of the mind, but not extreme elegance, delicacy, fineness, or breeding. Yes; my daughter is a good-looking girl and a good girl. Farewell! you will now ask me a thousand things about her, and why I said, " Poor Cecilia! what will become of her? " Very good! Do ask me; I have need to speak and no one here to whom I *can* speak of these things.

LETTER II

(The same)

Well, perhaps! a pretty Savoyard boy dressed as a girl. That is near enough. But do not forget, in order to imagine Cecilia as pretty as she is, a certain transparency in her complexion, something satiny, brilliant, which is given her by any slight heat; the contrary of anything dull or lifeless; the sheen of the red flower of the sweet pea. There you have my Cecilia! If you do not recognize her on meeting her in the street it will be your own fault.

You ask how it was that we got married when my husband and I had " only thirty-eight francs of fortune " between us; and you are astonished that, as I was an only child, I was not richer. The question is a strange one. People marry because they are men and women and attract one another. My father was a captain in the Dutch army. He lived on his pay and my mother's fortune, which was six thousand francs. My mother, I may say in passing, was of a bourgeois family in this town, but so pretty and amiable that my father never thought himself poor or ill-matched with her; and he loved her so tenderly that she died of sorrow at his death. Cecilia resembles her, not me or her father. May she have as happy a life as hers, but longer! My mother's six thousand francs were all my fortune; my husband's father gave each of his sons twenty thousand francs. The interest of our twenty-six thousand francs is enough to give us all the pleasures that we desire; but you see that Cecilia will not be married for her fortune. And yet it lay in my power to have her married.—No, it did not lie in my power; I could not have made up my mind to it, and she herself would not have wished it. Her suitor was a young minister, her relative on my mother's side, a little, pale, thin man, praised, petted, and pampered, by his whole family. They believe him, on account of a few bad verses, a little cold rhetoric, to be the greatest man of letters, the greatest genius, the greatest orator in Europe. We were at his parents' house, my daughter and I, about six weeks ago. A young lord and his tutor, who are staying there, passed the evening with us. After supper they all played " jeux d'esprit," then blind man's buff, then loto. The young Englishman is, as a man, much what my girl is as a woman; he is as pretty an English country lad as Cecilia is a pretty Vaudoise village girl. He did not shine at the " jeux d'esprit," but Cecilia had far more indulgence for his bad French than for the flat witticisms of her cousin, or, rather, to be more precise, she paid no attention at all to her cousin, but constituted herself the teacher and interpreter of the Englishman. At blind man's buff you can imagine that there was no comparison between the skill of the two young men; at loto the one was prudent and careful, the other absent and extravagant. Then it came to taking leave.

" Jeannot," said his mother, " you must escort
Cecilia; but it is cold, so put on your greatcoat,
and button it well up." His aunt brought him his
galoshes. While he was fastening himself up like
a portmanteau, as if in preparation for a long
journey, the young Englishman rushed up the
stairs four steps at a time, returned in a flash with
his hat, and offered Cecilia his arm. I could not
restrain my laughter, and I told her cousin that he
might unswaddle himself. If, up to then, his fate
with Cecilia had been doubtful, that moment
decided it. Although he is the only son of rich
parents and the heir to the fortunes of five or six
aunts, Cecilia will not marry her cousin the minister.

This mummy has a friend who is very much
alive, another young minister, who fell in love
with Cecilia after having seen her two or three
times at the house of his friend's mother. He is a
young man from the valley of the Lac du Joux,
handsome, fair, robust, who can walk ten leagues a
day, who shoots more than he studies, and who
goes every Sunday to preach at his chapel a league
away, in summer without a parasol, in winter
without galoshes or a greatcoat; he could carry,
if need were, his pedantic little friend on his arm.
If this husband were to suit my daughter I should
go very willingly to live with them in some
mountain parish; but his only fortune is his salary
as minister, and even that is not the chief difficulty.
I am afraid of the proverbial duplicity of mountain-
eers, for Cecilia I know could adjust herself to that

84

less easily than almoﬅ any woman; besides which, my brothers-in-law, her guardians, would never consent to such an alliance; and I myself indeed should only consent to it with regret.

LETTER III

(The same)

In addition to the two men of whom I have spoken, Cecilia has another suitor among the *bourgeoisie*, but he would more probably sink her to his position than rise to hers. He fights, drinks, and frequents women of the town like the German noblemen and young English gentlemen with whom he associates; he is otherwise amiable enough and very well in his person; but his charaﬅer alarms me. His idleness fatigues Cecilia; and although he has some fortune he may, through imitating those who have more, speedily find himself ruined.

There is yet another. He is a good young man, gentle and lovable; he has some talent and is devoted to business. Elsewhere he might make something of it, but here it is not possible. If my daughter felt a preference for him, and her uncles raised no obﬅacle, I would consent to go and live with them at Geneva, Lyons, or Paris, wherever they liked; but the young man does not perhaps love Cecilia enough to leave his native place, the most agreeable indeed which exists, or the view of our beautiful lake and its smiling shores. You see, my dear friend, that, among these four lovers there is not one husband. Neither is there one whom I could offer Cecilia in another cousin, very noble, very narrow, who inhabits a gloomy castle where they only read, from father to son, the Bible and the Gazette. "And the young lord?" you will ask. As to that there is a deal to be said. But it must keep for another letter. My daughter is urging me to walk out with her. Farewell.

LETTER IV

(The same)

Eight days ago, my cousin (the mother of the little theologian) being indisposed, we went to keep her company, my daughter and I. The young lord, when he heard of this, gave up a picnic which all the English at Lausanne were having that day, and asked my cousin to receive him. Except at meal-times he had not been seen there since the evening of the galoshes. He was greeted at first a little coldly; but he trod so delicately on tiptoe, spoke so low, was helpful with so good a grace, brought his French grammar so prettily to Cecilia, that she might teach him to pronounce, to say the words precisely as she did, that my cousin and her sisters soon softened; but all this displeased the son of the house just in proportion as it pleased the rest of the company, and he bore so much malice that, by dint of complaining of the noise they made overhead, which interrupted now his studies and now his sleep, he at length persuaded his kind, silly mother to request my lord and his tutor to look for another lodging. They came to tell me this yesterday, and to ask if I would take them to board. I refused very decidedly, without giving Cecilia time to conceive an idea or to form a wish. Then they limited their request to one for the use of a floor of my house which they knew to be empty. I still refused. " But only for two months," said the young man, " for one month, for fifteen days, until we have found some other lodging. I am not as noisy as Mr. S. says, but, even if I were so by nature, I am sure, madam, that you and mademoiselle your daughter would not hear me move, and, except for the favour of coming here sometimes to learn a little French, I should trouble you for nothing."

I looked at Cecilia; she had her eyes fixed on me. I saw clearly that I must refuse; but in truth I felt almost as much suffering as I caused. The tutor divined my reasons and checked the remonstrances of the young man, who has come this morning to tell me that, not having been able to persuade me to receive him at my house, he has lodged himself as close to us as possible, and to beseech permission to come and see us sometimes. I granted it. He then took his leave. After having accompanied him to the door Cecilia came and kissed me. "You are thanking me," I said. She blushed; I embraced her tenderly. Tears flowed from my eyes. She saw them, and I am sure that she read in them an exhortation to be wise and prudent, to her far more persuasive than the most eloquent discourse. But here are my brother-in-law and his wife; I am compelled to stop.

Everything is repeated, everything becomes known here in an instant. My brother-in-law has learned that I had refused to let for a very high price an apartment of which I made no use. He is my daughter's guardian. He, himself, lets apartments to strangers in his own house, sometimes even the whole of his house. Then he retires to the country and remains there. He therefore thought me very strange, and blamed me hugely. The only reason that I gave him was that it did not appear to me convenient to let. This fashion of answering seemed to him intolerably high. He was beginning indeed to get angry in earnest when Cecilia spoke up and said that I doubtless had reasons that I did not wish to give; that these reasons must be held to be good and that I ought not to be further pressed. I kissed her to thank her and saw the tears rise to her eyes. My brother- and sister-in-law withdrew without knowing what to think of either mother or daughter. I shall be blamed by the whole town. Cecilia alone will be on my side, and, perhaps, the young lord's governor.

You will comprehend very little doubtless of all this letting of houses, these ſtrangers, and the vexation shown by my brother-in-law. Do you know Plombières, or Bourbonne, or Barège? From what I have heard Lausanne is somewhat like these places. The beauty of our landscape, our Academy, and M. Tissot[1] bring us ſtrangers of all countries, of all ages, and of all charaſters, but not of all fortunes. Only the *rich* can live away from home. We have, therefore, above all, English gentlemen, French financiers, and German princes, who bring money to our inn-keepers, to the peasants of our neighbourhood, to our shop-keepers and artisans, and to those of us who have houses to let in the town or country, but who im-poverish all others by raising the price of food and labour, and by giving us a taſte for and an example of luxury little suited to our fortunes or our resources. The folk of Plombières, of Spa, or of Barège do not live with their gueſts or adopt their habits and cuſtoms. But we, whose society is more agreeable, and whose birth is not often inferior to theirs, we live with them, we please them, sometimes we form them, and they end by spoiling us. They turn the heads of our young girls, they make such of our young men as retain simple manners appear awkward and ſtiff, while such as have the absurdity to ape them often lose their fortune, and yet more often their health. Households and marriages are not the happier for

[1] A famous doſtor of Lausanne.

our having in our midst elegant French women, beautiful Englishwomen, handsome Englishmen, and amiable French rakes; and, even supposing that many marriages are not destroyed in this way, many are prevented. Young girls find that their compatriots lack elegance, young men think the girls coquettes. Both are afraid of the economies which marriage would oblige them to exercise, and, if indeed they feel any inclination, the one to have mistresses, the other lovers, nothing is more natural or reasonable than their apprehension of a narrow and hampered situation. Here is a very long letter! I am fatigued with writing. Farewell, dear friend.

LETTER V

(The same)

You are enchanted with Cecilia, and you have good reason to be. You ask me how I have contrived to make her so robust, to keep her so fresh and so healthy. I have always had her with me, she has always slept in my room and, when it was cold, in my bed. I love her above all things— that makes one very observant and far-seeing. You ask me if she has never been ill. You know that she has had the smallpox. I intended to have her inoculated but I was forestalled by the disease; it was long and violent. Cecilia is subject to severe headaches; every winter she has had chilblains on her feet which have sometimes compelled her to keep to her bed. I preferred that to hindering her from running about in the snow or warming herself afterwards when she was cold. As to her hands I was so afraid of their becoming ugly that I have succeeded in preventing it.

You ask how I have educated her. I have never had any other servant but a girl who was brought up at my grandmother's and who had served my mother. It was with her, in her village, at her niece's house, that I left Cecilia when I spent fifteen days with you at Lyons, and when I went to see you at your old aunt's. I taught my daughter to read and to write as soon as she was able to pronounce and to use her fingers; thinking, like the author of *Séthos*, that we only know well that which we have learned unconsciously. Between the ages of eight and sixteen years she took a daily lesson in Latin and in religion from her cousin, the father of her pedantic and jealous little cousin, and a music lesson from a very skilful old organist. I taught her as much arithmetic as a woman has need to know. I showed her how to sew, to knit, and to make lace. The rest I left to chance. She has learned a little geography by looking at the maps that hang in my ante-room, she has listened to what was being said when she was curious and when her attention was not inconvenient. I am not very learned; my daughter is still less so. I have not attempted always to occupy her; I permitted her to be dull when I did not know how to divert her. I gave her no expensive masters. She does not play the harp. She knows neither Italian nor English. She has only had dancing lessons during three months. You see that she is nothing very marvellous; but, in truth, she is so pretty, so good, and so natural, that I do not think anyone would wish her changed. Why, you will ask, did you have her taught Latin? In order that she should know French without my having to correct her continually, in order to occupy her, and for me to be free and able to rest for an hour every day; and then it cost me nothing. My cousin, the professor, had more wit than his son and all the simplicity that the latter lacks. He was an excellent man. He loved Cecilia, and, until his death, the lessons that he gave her were as agreeable to him as profitable to her. She nursed him during his last illness as she might have nursed her own father, and the example of patience and resignation that he gave her was a last lesson more important than all the rest. When she has the headache, when her chilblains prevent her from doing what she would wish, when there is any question of an epidemic threatening Lausanne (we are subject to epidemics), she remembers her cousin, the professor, and does not permit herself complaint, or impatience, or excessive fear.

You are very kind to thank me for my letters. It is for me to thank you for allowing me the pleasure of writing them.

LETTER VI

(The same)

" Was there no drawback," you ask me, " in permitting Cecilia thus to read and to listen? " " Would it not have been better, etc.? " I abbreviate, I do not transcribe all your observations, because they pained me. Perhaps it *would* have been better to have made her learn more, or less, or something different; perhaps there *was* some drawback, etc. But recollect that my daughter and I are not a romance, nor a moral lesson, nor an example to be cited. I loved my daughter above everything; nothing, it seems to me, divided my attention or weighed against her interests in my heart. After receiving your letter I sat down opposite to Cecilia; I watched her sewing with skill, activity, and animation. With my mind full of what you had written my eyes filled with tears; she began to play the piano to enliven me. I sent her to the other end of the town; she came and went without discomfort, although it was very cold. Some tedious visitors arrived; she was gentle, obliging, and gay. The young lord prayed her to accept a concert ticket; his offer pleased her but at a glance from me she refused it, with a very good grace. I am going to bed with an easy mind. I do *not* think I have brought her up badly. I am *not* going to reproach myself. The impression made by your letter is almost effaced. If my daughter is unhappy I shall be unhappy; but I shall not accuse myself. Nor shall I accuse my daughter; I shall accuse society, fate, or, rather, I shall accuse no one; I shall not complain, I shall submit in silence, with patience and courage. Do not make excuses for your letter; let us forget it. I know very well that you did not intend to pain me: you thought that you were discussing a book or questioning an author. To-morrow I will continue with a more tranquil mind.

Your husband does not think that I ought to complain of the strangers at Lausanne, because the number of people to whom they do good is larger than those to whom they do harm. That is possible, and I do *not* complain. Apart from this generous and sensible reason habit has made this gathering of strangers agreeable to us. It is gayer and more animated. It also appears to be a homage paid by the whole world to our charming country; the landscape itself can have no vanity, but *we* receive this homage with pride. Besides, who knows but that every girl does not secretly imagine a husband, every mother a son-in-law in each chaise that arrives? Cecilia has a new admirer who has not come from Paris or London. He is the son of our Governor, a fine young Bernese, pink and white, and the best fellow in the world. After having met us two or three times, I forget where, he began to visit us with some assiduity, and did not conceal from me that he kept his visits secret, so evident did it seem to him that his Bernese parents would be displeased if they saw their son becoming attached to a subject of the Pays-de-Vaud. Let him go on coming, poor boy, in secret or otherwise; he will do no harm either to Cecilia or to his own future; and neither Monsieur the Governor, nor Madame, will have any seduction to reproach us with. Here he is, in company with the young lord! I must leave you in order to receive them. Here are also the little dead-alive minister and the animated one. I am expecting the young scapegrace, and the young merchant, and many others. Cecilia is having a reception. A few young girls will come too, but they are less assiduous to-day than the young men. Cecilia has begged me to stay at home and to do the honours of her day, partly because she is more at ease when I am near her and partly because she thinks the air too cold for it to be prudent for me to go out.

LETTER VII

(The same)

You would desire me, in your admiration of Cecilia and your family pride, to banish the Governor's son from my house. You are wrong; you are unjust. The richest and best-born girl of the Pays-de-Vaud *is* a bad match for a Bernese who, by marrying at home, gains far more than fortune;

for he gains patronage and the means of entering the Government. He puts himself in the way of distinguishing himself, of making his talents useful to himself, his parents, and his country. I respect the fathers and mothers who feel this and who preserve their sons from the nets that might be spread for them here. Besides, a girl from Lausanne might well become the wife of a Governor, even of a Councillor, and still regret at Berne the lake of Geneva and its charming shores. It is as if a Parisian girl were to be turned into a princess in Germany. But I do wish that Bernese girls would more often marry men of the Pays-de-Vaud; that more equality and more frankness could be established between Berne and us, that we might cease complaining, sometimes unjustly, of Bernese pride, and that the Bernese would cease to give a shadow of reason to our complaints. . . .

Everything here appears to be unchanged; but I fear that my daughter's heart becomes daily more deeply touched. The young Englishman does not speak of love to her; I do not know if he feels it, but all his attentions are for her. She receives a fine bouquet on the days of the balls. He has taken her sleighing. It is with her that he always wishes to dance; it is to her or to me that he always offers his arm when we leave an assembly. She says nothing to me; but I see her contented or pensive according as she has seen him or not, according as his preference for her has been more or less marked.

Our old organist is dead. Cecilia has begged me
to employ the hour of her music lesson in teaching
her English. I have consented. She will know it
very soon. The young man is amazed at her
progress, and does not know that it is due to him.
People were beginning to make them play together
whenever they met; I did not wish her to play
cards. I said that a girl who played as ill as Cecilia
did wrong to play, and that I was sorry that she
had learned to play so young. Whereupon the
young Englishman had the smallest draught-
board made with the smallest possible draughts,
and now carries them always in his pocket. How
is one to prevent these children from playing?
When draughts fatigue Cecilia, he will procure, he
says, some little chessmen. He does not see how
little reason he has to fear her fatigue.

The young lord's governor, or rather he whom
I have called his governor, is his relative, of an
older but untitled branch of the same family. That
is what my lord told me. The other is not indeed
very much the elder and has in his countenance, in
his whole person, an indefinite charm such as I
have never before seen in any man.

Good God! how absorbed I am in what is
passing here and how perplexed as to what my
conduct should be! My lord's relative (I say my
lord, although there are many other lords, because
I do not wish to name him, and I do not wish to
name him for the same reason that causes me not
to sign my letters or name anyone—the mishaps

that may befall letters always alarming me); my
lord's relative is sad. I do not know whether it is
because of troubles that have afflicted him or
because of his natural disposition. He lives only
two steps away from us; he has taken to coming
every day, and, seated in the chimney-corner,
caressing my dog, reading the gazette or some
review, he allows me to attend to my house-
keeping, write my letters, or direct Cecilia's work.
He will correct, he says, her exercises, when she
can write them, and make her read the English
gazette in order to accustom her to the familiar and
spoken language. Ought I to dismiss him? Is it
not permissible for me, by letting him see what
mother and daughter are like from morning to
night, to persuade him to help in procuring a
brilliant and agreeable establishment for my
daughter—to oblige him to speak favourably of us
to the young man's father and mother? Must I
avoid that which might give Cecilia the man that
pleases her—I will not yet say the man she loves!
She will shortly be eighteen. Nature, perhaps,
even more than her heart. . . . Can one say of the
first woman to whom a man feels himself drawn,
that she is *loved* by him?

You would like me to have Cecilia taught
chemistry because in France all the young girls are
learning it. This reason does not appear to me
conclusive; but Cecilia, who hears it often talked
of, can read whatever she pleases on the subject.
As for me I do not like chemistry. I know that we

owe to chemists many discoveries and useful in-
ventions, and many interesting things; but their
proceedings give me no pleasure. I observe nature
as a lover; they study her as anatomists.

LETTER VIII

(The same)

Something occurred the other day which caused
me excessive emotion and alarm. I was reading,
and my Englishman was gazing silently into the
fire, when Cecilia returned from a visit she had
been paying, with her face white as death. I
was excessively alarmed. I asked her what was
the matter, what had happened to her. The
Englishman, almost as much distressed as I and
almost as pale as Cecilia, implored her to speak.
She would not say one word. He wished to withdraw, saying that it was undoubtedly his presence
that kept her from speaking; she held him back by
his coat and set to weeping or rather to sobbing.
I embraced her, I petted her, we gave her something to drink; still her tears flowed. Our silence
must have lasted more than half an hour. In order
to leave her more at her ease I had taken up my
work again, and he had begun to play with the dog.
At length she said to us, " It is very hard for me
to explain to you what has affected me so much,
and my own unhappiness vexes me more than its

cause. I do not know why I am troubled, and I am, above all, distressed at being so. What can it mean, mamma? Can you understand me when I cannot understand myself? I am, however, tranquil enough at this moment to tell you what is the matter. I will say it before this gentleman. He has taken too much trouble for me, he has shown me too much compassion for me to show him distrust. You may both quiz me if you like; perhaps I shall quiz myself; but, promise me, sir, to repeat what I tell you to no one."

" I promise you, mademoiselle," he said.

" Repeat to *no one?* "

" To no one."

" And you, mamma, never speak of it to me again unless I speak of it first. I saw my lord in the shop opposite. He was talking to Madame de X——'s waiting woman."

She said no more. We made her no answer. A moment later my lord entered.

He asked her if she would care to take a sleigh ride.

" No, not to-day," she said to him, " but to-morrow, if the snow lasts." Then, on going nearer to her, he remarked that her face was pale and her eyes swollen. He asked her what was the matter. His relative replied firmly that she could not tell him. He did not insist. He remained pensive, and a quarter of an hour later, some ladies having come in, they both went away. Cecilia composed herself fairly well. We did not again speak of anything in particular. Only on going to bed she said to me: " In truth, mamma, I do not know whether I desire the snow to melt or to hold." I did not answer her.

The snow melted; but they met afterwards as before. Cecilia has, however, seemed to me a trifle graver and more reserved. The waiting woman is pretty, so is her mistress. I do not know which of them was the cause of her uneasiness; but, since that moment I have been afraid that all this may become serious. I have not time to say more to-day, but I will soon write to you again.

LETTER IX

(The same)

You are very apprehensive over this Latin of Cecilia's and it seems to weigh on your mind.

" Do you know Latin? " you ask. No; but my father has told me a hundred times of his regret at not having made me learn it. He spoke French very well. He and my grandfather did not permit me to speak it too badly, and that is what makes me more fastidious than another. As to my daughter, one perceives, when she writes, that she knows her language, but she speaks sadly incorrectly. I let her talk. I like her inelegancies, either because they are hers, or because they are indeed pleasing.

She is more severe; if she sees me commit a fault of orthography, she catches me up. Her style is far more correct than mine; however, she writes as little as possible: it is too much trouble. So much the better. A love letter will not easily escape her pen. You ask if this Latin does not make her proud. Lord, no! What we learn in childhood does not appear to us to be stranger or more remarkable than breathing or speaking.

You ask how it is that I know English. Do you not recollect that we had an aunt who retired to England on account of her faith? Her daughter, my cousin, passed three years in my father's house during my youth, soon after my journey to Languedoc. She was a person of wit and parts. I owe her almost everything that I know, as well as my habits of study and thought. And now let us return to my favourite topic and customary particulars. Last week we were in an assembly when M. Tissot brought a Frenchwoman with a charming countenance, the finest eyes in the world, and all the grace that confidence added to familiarity with the world can give. She was dressed in the height of fashion, without being, for all that, absurd. An immense cadogan flowed below her shoulders and huge curls floated over her bosom. My lord and the young Bernese hovered around her continually, rather in amazement than in admiration; this at least is true of the Englishman, whom I observed attentively. Cecilia was also the centre of so much attention that, if she was affected by their desertion, she had no time to let it be seen. Only, when my lord wished to have his game of draughts, she said to him that, as she had a slight headache, she preferred not to play. She remained seated beside me all the evening, cutting out silhouettes for the child of the house. I do not know if the young lord knew what was passing in her mind, but, not knowing what to say to his Parisian lady, he went early away. When we left the room he was standing at the door among the servants. I do not know if Cecilia will ever again in all her life have so agreeable a moment!

Two days afterwards when he was passing the evening at my house together with his governor, the Bernese gentleman, and two or three young relatives of Cecilia, they began to discuss the French lady. The young men were merciless in their praise of her person, her eyes, her figure, her deportment, her dress. Finally they praised her forest of hair.

" Her hair is false," said Cecilia.

" Ha, Ha! Mademoiselle Cecilia," said the Bernese, " young ladies are all jealous of each other. Admit it. Is it not true that you are envious? "

It appeared to me that my lord smiled. I grew vexed in good earnest. " My daughter does not know what envy means," I said. " Like you she was praising the stranger's hair yesterday to a lady of my acquaintance, who was having her hair dressed. Her hairdresser, who had just left the

Parisian lady, said that the great cadogan and the great curls were false. If my daughter had been a little older she would have kept silence; at her age and having on her head a real forest it was natural enough to speak. Did you not maintain with vivacity yesterday," I continued, addressing myself to the Bernese, "that you had the largest dog in the country? And you, my lord, did you let us doubt that your horse was finer than this or that gentleman's?"

Cecilia, embarrassed, smiled and wept together.

"You are very good, mamma," she said, "to take my part so warmly. But at bottom I was in the wrong; it would have been better if I had kept silence. I was still out of humour."

"Sir," I said to the Bernese gentleman, "every time that a lady appears jealous of the praises you are bestowing on another, far from reproaching her, thank her in your heart, and think yourself flattered."

"I do not know," said my lord's relative, "if there is much reason to be. Women desire to please men, and men to please women; nature has thus ordained it. That we should wish to profit from the gifts we have received and not permit an usurper to enjoy them at our expense, appears to me so natural that I cannot see how it can be considered wrong. If another man were praised to these ladies for something I had done, assuredly I should say, ' It was I.' Besides, there is a certain spirit of veracity which, at the moment, does not regard either advantage or disadvantage. Supposing that Mademoiselle Cecilia wore false hair herself and that it had been admired, I am sure she would have said in the same manner, ' It is false.' "

" Undoubtedly, sir," said Cecilia, " nevertheless, I see very well that it was not fitting to say so about that of another lady."

At that moment chance brought us a young woman, together with her husband and brother. Cecilia sat down to her spinet, and played allemandes and country dances while they danced.

" Good-night, my mother and my protectress! " said Cecilia on retiring. " Good-night, my dear Don Quixote." I laughed.

Cecilia is forming and growing more amiable every day. May she not pay too dearly for these charms!

LETTER X

(The same)

I am much afraid that Cecilia has made a new conquest; and, if that is so, I should console myself, I think, for her preference for my lord. If it be indeed a preference only, it may not be a sufficient safeguard. The man in question is very agreeable. He is a gentleman of this country, a captain in the French service, who has just married, or, rather, has let himself be married, as ill as possible. He had no fortune. A distant relative of the same name, the heiress to a fine property that has been for long in the family, said she would marry him as willingly as another. His parents thought it an admirable plan, and believed the girl to be charming merely because she is lively, and bold, speaks fast and a great deal, and passes for a wit. He was then in garrison. They wrote to him. He replied that he had had no intention of marrying at present, but would do as they wished; and things were so promptly arranged that, arriving here on the first of October he found himself married by the twentieth. I believe that by the thirtieth he wished he were not. The lady is coquettish, jealous, and proud. What she flaunts as wit is in truth only vivacious and pretentious folly. I went, without Cecilia, to compliment the pair two months ago. They have now been fifteen days in the town. Madam would like to take part in every gaiety, to shine and please, and play a part. She is rich, pleasing, and pretty enough for that.

The husband, embarrassed and dull, flies from his own house, and, as we are slightly related, it is in mine that he seeks refuge. The first time that he came he was struck with Cecilia, whom he had only seen as a child, and finding me almost always alone with her, or only the Englishman with us, he formed the habit of coming every day. These two men suit and please each other. Both are cultivated, both have delicacy and wit, discrimination and taste, politeness and sensibility. My relative is indolent and lazy; he is no longer so unhappy at being married because he has almost forgotten that he is so. The other is quietly sad and pensive. Since the first day they have associated with as much ease as if they had known each other all their lives; but my relative appears to me each day to be more occupied with Cecilia. Yesterday, while they were speaking of America and of the war, Cecilia said to me quite low, " Mamma, one of these gentlemen is in love with you."

" And the other with you," I answered.

Whereupon she set to surveying him, smiling. He is of so noble and distinguished an appearance that were it not for the young lord I should be concerned to think I had spoken a truth. Indeed, I ought still to feel concerned; but it is not possible to take so many things at once to heart. My relative and his wife must extricate themselves as best they can. My cousin has not observed the young lord, who is not here as much as his governor, but when the young man, on returning from his college and his studies, does not find his companion at his own house he comes to look for him at mine. That is what he did yesterday; and, knowing that we were to go that evening to the cousin with whom he had been boarding, he implored me to conduct him there, saying that he could not endure, after the kindnesses he had met with at first in that family, the appearance of coolness that now existed between them. I said that

I was quite agreeable. The two pillars of my hearth also accompanied us. My cousin, the professor's wife, convinced that, in any contest of wit, her son would always shine more brightly than anyone else, set us first to playing at "bouts rimés," then to word games, and finally to writing questions upon cards. These cards were then shuffled, each of us drew one at hazard and wrote an answer beneath the question. Then they were shuffled again and everybody wrote until the cards were filled. To me was committed the task of reading them out loud. There were some excessively stupid sayings and others that were extremely neat. On one of the cards there was written: " To whom does one owe one's first education? "

" To one's nurse," was the reply.

Under the reply was written, " And the second? "

Answer, " To chance."

" And the third? "

" To love."

" Was it you who wrote that? " said one of the company to me.

" I am willing," I replied, " that you should think so; for it is very neat."

Monsieur de X—— looked at Cecilia. " She who wrote it," he said, " owes already much to her third education."

Cecilia coloured as she had never done before.

" I should like to know who really wrote it," said the young lord.

"Was it not you yourself?" I asked. "Why must it have been a woman? Have not you men as much need of this third education as we have? It was perhaps my young cousin, the minister."

"Speak up, Jeannot," said his mother. "I could easily think it was you, for it is so clever."

"Oh no," said Jeannot, "I finished *my* education at Basle."

That brought a laugh, and the game came to an end.

When we returned home Cecilia said to me: "It was not I, mamma, who wrote that answer."

"Why then those blushes?" I asked.

"Because I thought . . . because mamma— because . . ."

I learned, or at least she told me no more.

LETTER XI

(The same)

You wish to know whether Cecilia has divined truly concerning my friend the Englishman. I do not know, I do not think about it, I have not the leisure to consider it.

Yesterday we attended a great assembly at the castle. A nephew of the governor, who had arrived the day before, was presented by him to such ladies as he desired to distinguish. I have never seen a man of finer appearance. He serves in the same regiment as my relative. They are friends; and on seeing the latter speaking with Cecilia and me, he joined in the conversation. I was vastly pleased. No one could possibly be more polite, speak more agreeably, have a more elegant address and air, or nobler manners. This time it was the turn of the young lord to be troubled. He appeared to be no more than a pretty boy of no consequence. I do not know if he felt anxious, but he kept very close to us. As soon as there was any question of sitting down to cards he asked me if it would be proper to play at draughts at the governor's, as in other houses, and implored me, if I did not think it proper, to contrive in such a manner that he might play at *reversi* with Cecilia. He pretended to know only her in all the company, and to play so badly that he would vex any ladies with whom he might be set at cards. In proportion as the two most striking men in the assembly appeared occupied with my daughter he seemed the more proud of his connection with her. He did in truth pay more attention to her than usual. It seemed to me that she observed this; but instead of laughing at him, as he deserved, she appeared to me to be well pleased. Happy in making a favourable impression on her lover she liked even the cause of it.

You are surprised that Cecilia goes out alone and is permitted to receive in my absence both young men and young women; I even see that you blame me in this respect; but you are in the wrong. Why not permit her to enjoy a liberty that our customs sanction, and which she is so little tempted to abuse? For, circumstances having separated her from the companions whom she had in her childhood, Cecilia has but one intimate friend, her mother, and leaves me as little as possible. We have here some mothers who, from prudence or vanity, bring up their daughters as young ladies of rank are brought up in Paris; but I do not see what they gain by it, and as I hate useless restrictions and detest pride, I have been careful not to imitate them. Cecilia is related to the relatives of my mother as well as to those of my husband; she has cousins in every quarter of our town, and I think it right that she should associate with all of them, according to our customs, and that she should be beloved by them all. In France, I should do as is done in France; here you would act as I do. Heaven! how odious and ridiculous a little person appears to me who is proud and supercilious, and who measures her greeting, her tone, her curtsey, according to the importance of the persons she meets! Ever in fear of compromising itself, this humble vanity (as I may term it) would seem to own that a trifle would suffice to degrade its dignity. It is a quality not rare in our small towns, and I have seen enough of it to disgust me.

LETTER XII

(The same)

If you did not press me with so much kindness and insistence to continue my letters, I should hesitate to-day. Until now I have derived pleasure and have refreshed myself by writing. To-day I fear the contrary. In addition, to render my narrative precise, a letter would be required that I cannot write from memory. . . . Ah! here it is, it lay in a corner of my desk! Cecilia, who has gone out, doubtless feared that it might fall from her pocket. I must copy it, for I should not dare send it you. She might perhaps one day wish to re-read it. This time you should indeed thank me. I am imposing upon myself an odious task.

Since the moment of jealousy of which I told you, whether she was sometimes in ill humour and had retained some suspicions, or whether, having seen more clearly into her own heart, she had condemned herself to more reserve, Cecilia would no longer play at draughts with my lord in company. She sewed and watched me play. But at my house they did play once or twice, and the young man set himself the other evening to show her the moves at chess while his relative and mine (I mean the officer) were playing at piquet together. Seated between the two tables I was working and watching them play, sometimes the two men, sometimes the two children, who that evening had

more the appearance of children than usual; for
my daughter mistook continually the names and
the moves of the chessmen, thus giving rise to
pleasantries that made up in gaiety what they
lacked in wit. Once the young lord became impatient with her inattention and Cecilia grew
vexed at his impatience. I turned my head. I saw
that both of them were sulking. I shrugged my
shoulders. A moment later, not hearing them
speak, I looked at them. Cecilia's hand lay immovable on the chessboard. Her head was bent
forward and bowed. The young man, bent towards
her, appeared to be devouring her with his eyes.
It was total absorption, ecstasy, abandonment.

" Cecilia," I said gently, for I did not wish to
startle her, " Cecilia, what are you thinking of? "

" Nothing," she said, hiding her face in her
hands, and pushing her chair brusquely back. " I
think these wretched chessmen are tiring me.
During these last minutes, my lord, I distinguish
them even less well than before, and you will have
even more reason to complain of your pupil; let
us leave them." And, in fact, she rose, quitted the
room, and did not return until I was alone. Then
she knelt down, rested her head upon me, and
taking both my hands, moistened them with her
tears.

" What is it, my Cecilia? " I asked, " what is
it? "

" It is I who am asking that, mamma," she said.
" What is it that is happening to me? What is it

that I am feeling? What am I ashamed of? At what am I weeping?"

"Has he observed your emotion?" I asked her.

"I do not think so, mamma," she replied. "Repenting, maybe, his impatience, he pressed and kissed the hand with which I was trying to lift a fallen pawn. I withdrew my hand; but I felt so happy that our disagreement was ended, his eyes appeared to me so tender, I was so much moved! At that very moment you said softly: 'Cecilia!' He may perhaps have thought that I was still sulking, for I was not looking at him."

"I hope so," I said.

"I also hope so," she replied. "But, mamma, why do *you* hope it?"

"Are you ignorant, my dear Cecilia," I asked, "of men's readiness to speak and to think evil of women?"

"But," said Cecilia, "if there is any occasion here for evil speaking or thinking he could not accuse me without even more accusing himself. Did he not kiss my hand and was he not as troubled as I was?"

"Perhaps, Cecilia; but he will not recollect his emotion as he will recollect yours. He will see in yours a degree of sensibility or weakness that may carry you far and decide your fate. His emotion is doubtless not new to him, and is not of so much consequence to him. Absorbed still in your image, should he have met a light woman in the street? . . ."

" Ah, mamma! "

" Yes, Cecilia; you muſt not cherish these illusions; a man seeks to inspire in every woman, for himself alone, a sentiment that he himself has moſt commonly only for the sex. Finding everywhere that with which to satisfy his inclination, what is moſt often the great affair of our life may be scarcely anything to him."

" The great affair of our life! What! It happens to women to think much of a man who thinks but little of them? "

" Yes; that happens. It happens also to some women to think much, despite themselves, of men in general. Whether they yield or whether they resiſt this inclination it remains the great, the sole affair of these unhappy women. Cecilia; in your religious lessons you were told that you muſt be chaſte and pure: did you attach any meaning to those words? "

" No, mamma."

" Well! the moment has come for you to praᵭise a virtue, to abſtain from a vice of which you can form no idea. If this virtue appears difficult to you, remember that it is the only one which you will have to prescribe to yourself with rigour or to praᵭise with vigilance, with scrupulous watchfulness over yourself."

" The only one? "

" Examine yourself, and read the Decalogue. Have you any need to watch over yourself in order not to kill, not to deceive, not to slander?

You have certainly never recollected that all that
was forbidden you.   You will never need to
recollect it; and if you have ever an inclination to
covet anything, it also will be the lover or the
husband of another woman, or perhaps the
advantages that the husband or the lover whom
you desire for yourself may give to another woman.
That which is called *virtue* in woman is perhaps the
only one that you could fail to have, the only one
which you could practise *as* a virtue, the only one
of which you could say in practising it: ' I am
obeying the precepts that I am told are God's laws,
and which I have received as such.' "

" But, mamma, have not men received the same
laws? Why do they permit themselves to neglect
them, and to make their observance so difficult to
us? "

" I scarcely know, Cecilia, what to answer you:
but that does not really concern us.   I have no son.
I do not know what I should say to a son.   I have
only thought about the daughter that I have got,
and whom I love above everything.   What I can
say to *you* is that society which dispenses men and
does not dispense women from a law which
religion appears to have given equally to both
alike, imposes upon men other laws which are,
perhaps, not easier to observe.   It exacts from
them reserve, even in disorder; delicacy, discretion, and courage; and, if they forget these
laws, they are dishonoured, people avoid them,
their company is shunned, they find everywhere a

reception which says: ' You were given sufficient privileges and were not content with them; society will intimidate, by your example, those who might be tempted to imitate you, and who, in imitating you, would trouble everything, overset everything, and remove from the world all security and all confidence.' And such men, although they may be punished more severely than ever women are, have often been guilty only of imprudence, of weakness, or of a moment of frenzy; for men of determined vice, the really wicked, are as rare as perfeƈt men or perfeƈt women. These exiƒt only in indifferent romances. I do not find, I repeat, the position of men to be, even in this respeƈt, so very different from that of women. And then, how many other painful obligations does not society impose on them? Do you think, for inƒtance, that should war be declared, it would be very agreeable to your cousin to leave us in the month of March in order to expose himself to the danger of being killed or crippled, or, through sleeping on wet ground, to the risk of taking the germs of a perhaps incurable disease? "

" But mamma, it is his duty, his profession; he has chosen it. He is paid for all that you have juƒt described; and if he diƒtinguishes himself he will win honour, even perhaps a laƒting fame. He will be promoted; he will be honoured wherever he goes, in Holland, in France, in Switzerland, even amongƒt the very enemies whom he has fought."

" Well, Cecilia; it is the duty, it is the profession

of every woman to be virtuous. She has not chosen it, but most men have not chosen *their* profession. Their parents, circumstances, usually make this choice for them before they are of an age to judge or to choose. A woman also is repaid by the fact that she *is* a woman. Are we not almost entirely dispensed from heavy work? Do not men protect us against heat, cold, and fatigue? And are there many men so impolite as not to cede to us the best pavement, the least stony path, the most comfortable place? If a woman permits no slur on her conduct, on her reputation, she must be in other respects very odious, very disagreeable, not to find consideration everywhere; and then, is it nothing, after having attracted a good man, to fix him, to be chosen by him and by his parents to be his companion? Imprudent girls please even more than others; but it is rare that a man's infatuation goes so far as marriage and even rarer that, after marriage, a humiliating repentance does not punish the woman for her seductiveness. Dearest Cecilia! one moment of that sensibility to which I did not wish you to yield, has often caused girls who were amiable and not vicious, to lose an advantageous establishment and the hand of the man whom they loved and who loved them."

"What! This sensibility that they inspire, that they seek to inspire, estranges men?"

"It frightens them, Cecilia; up to the moment when there is a question of marriage men wish

their mistress to be tender, and complain if she be
not sufficiently so.   But when marriage is in
question, supposing that his head is not quite
turned, the man judges as if he were already a
husband, and a husband is a thing so different from
a lover that the one judges nothing as did the other.
Refusals are recollected with pleasure, favours
with uneasiness.   The confidence that too tender
a girl has shown appears no more than an imprudence which she might commit with any man who
invited it.   The too lively sensibility awakened by
the attentions of her lover now appear only as an
inclination to love any man.   Judge then the dis-
pleasure, the jealousy, the mortification of the
husband; for the desire of exclusive possession is
the most lively sentiment that remains to him.   He
might console himself for being loved but little
provided that no one else were loved at all.   He is
jealous even when he has ceased to love, and his
uneasiness is not as absurd, as unjust, as you
might at present imagine.   I often think men
odious in what they exact from women, and in the
manner in which they exact it; but I do not think
them so greatly mistaken in fearing what they fear.
An imprudent girl is seldom a prudent or good
wife.   She who has not resisted her lover before
marriage is seldom true to him afterwards.   Often
she no longer sees the lover in the husband.   The
one is as negligent as the other was attentive.   The
one found everything right, the other finds almost
everything wrong.   She scarcely feels obliged to

keep to the second the troth that she swore to the first. Her imagination may also have promised her pleasures which she has not found, or no longer finds. She hopes to find them elsewhere than in marriage; and if she has not resisted her inclinations as a girl, she will not resist them as a woman. The habit of compliance will have been formed, duty and modesty already accustomed to yield. That which I say is so true that the world admires the virtue of a beautiful woman courted by many men as much as the reserve of a girl in the same situation. It is recognized that the temptation is almost the same and resistance as difficult. I have seen women marry under the influence of the strongest passion and have a lover two years after marriage, then another, then another, until despised, degraded . . ."

"Oh, mamma," cried Cecilia, rising, "have I deserved all this?"

"You mean, ' Have I need of all this? ' " I said, drawing her on to my knees and drying on my face the tears which were streaming over hers. "No, Cecilia; I do not think that you *have* need of so shocking a picture, and, if you *had* need of it would you be the more guilty, would you be less estimable, less amiable? Would you be less dear or less precious to me? But go to bed, my child; go, believing that I blame you for nothing, and that it was necessary to warn you. Just this once I have warned you. Go!"—and she went.

I sat down to my desk and I wrote:

" My Cecilia, my dear daughter, I have promised
you that only this once will you be tormented by
the anxiety of a mother who loves you more than
life itself; in future, knowing on the subject all
that I myself know, all that I have ever thought,
my daughter can judge for herself. I may *remind*
her sometimes of what I have said to-day, I shall
never *repeat* it. Allow me therefore to continue,
Cecilia; and be attentive to the end. I shall not
say to you what I would say to many others;
that, if you fail in prudence you will renounce all
the virtues; that, jealous, deceitful, coquettish,
inconstant, soon loving yourself alone, you will be
neither daughter, friend, nor lover. I shall tell
you on the contrary that the precious qualities that
you possess and that you will never lose, will
make the loss of that one virtue more regrettable,
and will increase the misfortune and the disadvantages.

" Sincere, humble, just, you would dishonour
only more certainly those whose honour depended
on your virtue. Disorder would surround you.
If your husband had a mistress you would think
yourself happy to share with her an establishment,
in which you would no longer feel yourself to have
any rights, and perhaps you would even permit her
children to share the patrimony of yours. Be wise,
my Cecilia, in order to enjoy your amiable qualities. Be wise, my Cecilia; you will expose yourself otherwise to too great unhappiness.

" Profit, if you can, by my advice; but, if you

do *not* follow it, never hide yourself from a mother who adores you. What would you have to fear? Reproaches? I should make none; they would pain me more than you. The loss of my affection? I should perhaps only love you the more when you were to be pitied, and when you were running the risk of being abandoned by the world. To make me die of grief? No! I should live, I should endeavour to live, to prolong my life in order to soften the sorrows of yours, to oblige you to esteem yourself in spite of weaknesses that would leave you in my eyes a thousand virtues and a thousand charms."

Cecilia, on waking, read what I had written. I summoned some sewing-women of whom we had need. I endeavoured to distract and occupy both Cecilia and myself, and I succeeded. But, after dinner, while we were working together with the sewing-women, she broke silence.

" One word, mamma. If husbands are what you have painted them, if marriage is worth so little, would the loss be so great? "

" Yes, Cecilia: you see how sweet it is to be a mother. Besides, there are exceptions, and every girl, thinking that her lover and herself would have proved exceptional, regrets his loss as a great misfortune, when it might have been nothing of the kind."

The young lord came that day to see us earlier than was his custom. Cecilia scarcely lifted her eyes from her work. She excused herself for her inattention of the day before, said it was very natural that he should have become impatient, and blamed herself for having shown ill-humour. She begged him, after having asked my permission, to return the next day to give her a lesson of which she intended to profit far more than before.

" What! It is *that* which you remember? " he said, going nearer to her and pretending to examine her work.

" Yes," she said, " it is that."

" I dare to hope," he said, " that you have not been angry with me."

" Not at all," she answered.

He went out, undeceived, or rather, deceived indeed.

Cecilia wrote on a card: " I have misled him, but it is not very agreeable to have to do so."

I wrote: " No, but it was necessary, and you have done well. I am at one with you, Cecilia. I wish that this marriage lay in your hands. My lord's parents would not be greatly pleased, but as they would be in the wrong, that does not trouble me excessively. You must therefore try to deceive him. If you succeed in misleading him he may say: ' She is an amiable girl, good, not very susceptible with that kind of susceptibility to be feared by a husband; she will be prudent, I love her, I will marry her.' If you do not succeed, if he sees through your reserve, he may say: ' She knows how to conquer herself, she is prudent, I love her, I esteem her, I will marry her.' "

123

Cecilia gave me back the two cards, smiling.

"Mamma," said she, "say anything that you like to me; but as to reminding me of what you have already said or written, there is no need: I *could* not forget it. I have not understood it all, but the words are printed on my brain. I shall explain to myself what you have said by the things that I see and read, and these in their turn will be explained by what you have said. It will all become clear together."

The young lord came that evening as she had asked him. The game of chess went very well. My lord said to me in the course of it: "You will think me very strange, madam; I complained two days since that mademoiselle was not sufficiently attentive, this evening I find her too much so." In his turn he was absent and dreamy. Cecilia appeared to notice nothing. If she continues thus I shall admire her. Good-bye; I repeat that which I said at the beginning of my letter; this time you do owe me thanks. I have fulfilled my task even better than I thought possible. I have copied my letter and our notes, I have remembered what was said almost word for word.

LETTER XIII

(The same)

Everything goes on well enough. Cecilia conducts herself with great prudence. The young man looks at her occasionally with an air that seems to say: " Was I then in error and am I in truth indifferent to you? " Each day he grows more diligent in his efforts to please. We do not now see anything either of my cousin, the young minister, nor of his friend the mountaineer. The young Bernese, feeling himself perhaps too much eclipsed by his cousin, no longer honours us with his visits. But his cousin comes to see us very often and always appears to me very amiable. As to the other two men I call them my household gods.

I am very glad that you are so pleased with Cecilia. You consider me extremely indulgent and you do not know why I am so; in truth neither do I. There would not have been, it appeared to me, either justice or prudence in greater serenity. How should a girl protect herself from an emotion that she has neither experienced nor imagined? Is there any law, natural or revealed, human or divine, which says: " The first time that your lover kisses your hand you are not to be agitated? " Should I have threatened her with

" des chaudières bouillantes
Où on plonge en jamais les femmes mal-vivantes "?

125

Should I, in showing disapprobation or in avoiding her, have given her reason to say, as in *Télémaque*: " Oh, my lord! as mamma abandons me, no one remains but you." Supposing anyone *were* lunatick enough to say to me " Yes; you *should* have acted in that manner," I should reply that, having neither indignation nor disapproval in my heart, such behaviour, which would not have seemed to me either just or prudent, would also not have been possible.

LETTER XIV

(The same)

What will you think of an occurrence that agitated us yesterday, my daughter and I, to such a degree that we have scarcely opened our mouths to-day, not wishing to speak of it and not being able to speak of anything else. At least that is what closes my mouth and I think it is what closes Cecilia's. She still looks alarmed. For the first time in her life she has slept badly, and I find her very pale.

Yesterday, as my lord and his relative were dining at the Castle, we had, after dinner, only my military cousin. My daughter requested him to make a point to her pencil. He took a penknife; the wood of the pencil was hard, his knife very sharp. He cut his hand deeply, and the blood flowed with such abundance that I was alarmed. I ran to look for some English plaister, a bandage, and some water. "It is strange," he said smiling, "and absurd, but I feel very faint." He was seated. Cecilia said that he grew very pale. I called from the door: "My child, you have some Eau-de-Cologne." She quickly moistened her handkerchief and with one hand she held this handkerchief, which hid Monsieur de X——'s face from her, while with the other she endeavoured to stop the blood with her apron. She thought him almost fainting, she said, when she felt him draw her towards him. Bent forward as she was she could not have resisted; but fear and surprise removed all power of movement. She thought him mad, she thought that a convulsion had caused him to make an involuntary movement, or rather, she thought nothing, so rapid and confused were her ideas. He said to her: "Dear Cecilia; charming Cecilia!" At that very moment that he was pressing with transport a kiss upon her forehead, or rather, upon her hair (from the manner in which she was bent over him), I re-entered the chamber. He rose, permitting her to take his place. His blood was still flowing. I summoned our maid Fanchen, showed her my relative's hand, and gave her the remedies I had brought. Then, without saying a single word, I took my daughter away. More dead than alive she recounted to me that which I have just told to you.

"Mamma," she said, "how could I fail to have

the presence of mind to throw myself to one side,
or to turn my head away? I had two hands, he
only one. I did not make the slightest effort to
disengage myself from his arm which was round
my waist and was pulling me. I continued to hold
my apron round his wounded hand. What did it
matter whether he bled a little more or less? He
must have formed a strange opinion of me! Is it
not terrible to lose one's judgment at the very
moment that one needs it most?"

I made no reply. Fearing equally to engrave too
deeply on her imagination something which
caused her so much pain, and to make her regard
it as a common occurrence to which she need not
attach too much importance, I did not dare to
reply. I made Fanchen say at the door that Cecilia
was indisposed. We passed the evening together
reading English history. She now understands
Robertson fairly well. The story of the unhappy
Queen Mary interested her a little, but from time
to time she said: "But mamma, was it not all very
strange? Was he mad?"

"Something very like it," I answered; "but
read, my child, that will distract both you and me."

Suddenly he appeared. He did not have himself
announced, for fear, doubtless, of being sent away.
I did not know how to speak to him, how to look
at him, and I occupied myself with some letters.
Then I saw Cecilia make him a low curtsey. He
was as pale as she was, and did not appear to have
slept any better. I could not proceed with my

letters. I could not leave my daughter any longer in embarrassment. . . .

Monsieur de X—— drew nearer to me when he saw me lay down my pen.

" Do you intend to banish me from your house, madam? " he asked. " I do not know myself if I have really deserved so cruel a punishment. I am guilty, it is true, of the most unpardonable, the most inconceivable lack of control, but of no ill design, indeed, of *no* design. Did I not know that you were about to come back? I love Cecilia; I say it to-day as an excuse, and yesterday, when I came to you, I thought never to have said it without being guilty of a crime. I love Cecilia, and I was not able to feel her hand on my face, and my hand in hers, without, for the moment, losing my reason. Speak now, madam, do you banish me from your house? Mademoiselle, do you banish me, or will you both pardon me generously? If you will *not* pardon me I shall leave Lausanne this evening. I shall say that one of my friends has asked me to take his place in the regiment. It would be impossible to me to live here if I could not come to you, or to come if I were received as you must think I deserve to be."

I did not reply. Cecilia then asked my leave to reply. I said that I agreed beforehand to whatever she should decide.

" I forgive you, sir," she said, " and I beg my mother to forgive you. At bottom it is my fault. I should have been more circumspect, have given

you my handkerchief and not held it, have detached
my apron after wrapping your hand in it.   I did not
know the possible consequences; behold me enlightened for the rest of my life!   But, since *you*
have made a confession, I shall now make one also
which may perhaps be helpful to you, and which
will doubtless make you understand why I do not
fear to continue to see you.   I also have a preference for someone."

" What! " he exclaimed, " You are in love? "

Cecilia did not reply.   I have never in my life
been so agitated.   I had suspected it; but to *know*
it! to know that she is enough in love to confess it,
and to confess it thus, knowing that it is a protection to her and that other men are not to be
feared by her!   Monsieur de X——, on whom my
eyes fell, made me pity him at that moment, and I
forgave him everything.

" The man whom you love, mademoiselle," he
asked, in a changed voice, " does he know his
happiness? "

" I flatter myself that he has not divined my
sentiments," answered Cecilia, in the softest voice
and with the most modest expression that I have
ever seen on her countenance.

" But how is that possible? " he asked.   " For,
loving you, he must study your slightest words,
your slightest actions, and thus must he not have
guessed? "

" I do not know that he loves me," interrupted
Cecilia, " he has not told me so, and it seems to me

that I should perceive it, for the very reasons that you yourself have stated."

" I should like to know," he continued, " who is the man so happy as to please you, so blind as not to observe it? "

" And why would you like to know? " asked Cecilia.

" It seems to me," he said, " that I should not bear him any ill-will, because I do not believe him to be as much in love as I am. I should speak so much of you to him, and with so much passion, that he would pay closer attention to you, that he would appreciate you better, and would place his fate in your hands; for I cannot believe him to be as unhappily bound as I am. I should have at least the happiness of serving you, and I should find some consolation in thinking that another could not be as happy as I should have been in his place."

" You are generous and amiable," I said, " I, too, forgive you with all my heart."

He wept and so did I. Cecilia bent her head and took up her work again.

" Had you told your mother? " he asked.

" No," I said, " she had not told me."

" But you know who it is? "

" Yes, I guess."

" And if you cease to love him, mademoiselle? "

" Do not wish that," she said, " you are so amiable that, in such a case, I should have to banish you."

Some visitors came in, and he made his escape.

I told Cecilia to remain with her back turned to the window, and I had some coffee brought which I asked her to serve, although it was not at all the hour for drinking it. That business afforded her occupation and protection so that she had to answer very few questions about her pallor or her indisposition of the previous day. There was only our friend the Englishman, whom nothing escapes.

"I have met your relative," he said to me in a low voice. "He would have avoided me if it had been possible. What an air he had! Ten days of sickness could not have changed him more than he is changed since yesterday.

"'You find me very pale?' he said. 'Is it not strange,' and he showed me his hand, 'that a mere prick, although in truth a deep one, should have affected me thus.'

"I asked him where he had thus pricked himself. He said that it was at your house, with a penknife while cutting a pencil; that he had lost a quantity of blood and had felt faint.

"'It is so absurd,' he said, 'that I blush for it.' And in truth he did blush and appeared only the paler a moment later. I saw that he spoke the truth, but not the whole truth. On coming here I find you with an air of emotion and sensibility. Miss Cecilia is pale and dejected. Allow me to ask what has occurred."

"Because you were my confidant once," I replied, smiling, "you would like to be it always;

but there are things which one cannot discuss," and we then spoke of other matters.

Our guests worked, supped, played at piquet, at whist, at chess, as usual. The game of chess was very serious. The Bernese gentleman was teaching Cecilia how to play according to " Philidor," which manual I had procured for her. My lord, whom that did not at all amuse, had relinquished his usual place and had asked if he might join in a rubber of whist. At the close of the evening, seeing Cecilia sewing, he said to her: " You have refused me all the winter, mademoiselle, a purse or a pocket-book. I must, however, now when I am going away, take with me a ' souvenir ' of you and you must permit me to leave you one of me."

" By no means, my lord," she replied; " if we are never to meet again we should do much better to forget each other."

" You have great firmness, mademoiselle," he said, " and you say ' never meet again ' as if you were saying nothing of consequence."

I had drawn near to them so I now broke in: " There is firmness indeed in Cecilia's phrase; but you, my lord, have it in your mind, which is far more admirable."

" I, madam? "

" Yes; when you spoke of departure and ' souvenir ' you were certainly thinking of an eternal separation."

" That is quite certain," said Cecilia, forcing herself for the first time in her life to put on an air of pride and indifference. What is more I believe that if the indifference was only in her air the pride was in her heart. The tone in which he had said, " when I go away " had wounded her. He now was wounded in his turn.

" What a day! " said Cecilia, as soon as we were alone. " May I ask you, mamma, what has most affected you? "

" Your words: ' I also have a preference for someone.' "

" I was not then mistaken," she pursued after embracing me; " but do not fear, mamma. There seems to me that there is nothing to fear. I find in myself, as he says, firmness, and then I wish so earnestly not to give you pain! This morning you know that we scarcely spoke at all. Well! During that silence I was considering the kind of life which, with your consent, we might perhaps lead for a short time. It may be a little inconvenient for you and very distasteful to me; but I know that you would do for me things that were far more difficult."

" How would you like us to live, Cecilia? "

" It appears to me that it would be more prudent for us to stay less at home and for those three or four men to find us less often alone. The life which we are leading is so sweet for me and so agreeable for them; you are so amiable, mamma; we are too comfortable, nothing troubles us, we think and act just as we choose. It would be better, at the risk of tedium, to go more into society. You can desire me to learn to play cards, and thus there will be no more question of chess or draughts. We shall all become a little less indispensable to each other. If there is any question of love it can easily be shown and at length confessed. If there is not it will be seen more clearly and I shall not be able to deceive myself any longer."

I pressed her to my heart. " How amiable, how reasonable you are! " I exclaimed. " How content and satisfied I am with you! Yes, my child, we shall do all that you desire. Let no one ever reproach me with my weakness or blindness. How could you have been what you now are, if my mind had been yours, and if, instead of having a soul of your own, you had only had mine? You are better than I am. I see in you qualities which I thought almost impossible to unite, as much firmness as sensibility, discernment as simplicity, prudence as uprightness. May this sentiment, which has developed such rare qualities in you, not make you pay too dearly for the good it has done you! May it perish or bring you happiness! "

Cecilia, who was excessively tired, begged me to undress her, help her to go to bed, and then have my supper at her bedside. In the middle of supper she fell asleep. It is eleven o'clock and she is not yet up. From to-night onwards I shall begin to execute her plan and I shall relate to you in a few days with what success.

LETTER XV

(The same)

We are living according to Cecilia's wishes, and I am greatly diverted by the manner in which we are welcomed to a society that we had previously neglected. We are a species of novelty. Cecilia, who has gained countenance, sufficient ease of manner, obligingness, and frankness is certainly a very agreeable novelty; and, what is of more importance than all this, we give back to society four men whom it is not unwilling to receive. The first times that Cecilia played whist her Bernese admirer desired to be her master as he had been at chess, and the assiduity which he showed kept the young lord at a distance. The idea which folk had had at the beginning of the winter that my lord must always be set to play with her forthwith disappeared and we had in one day some absurd and some diverting scenes.

Cecilia had been dining with a rich relative and I was alone at three o'clock when my lord and his cousin came in.

" One must come very early in order to hope to find you," said my lord. " Before this change we had six weeks which were far more agreeable than these last eight or ten days. May I be permitted to ask, madam, whether it is you or Miss Cecilia who wishes to go out every day? "

" It is my daughter," I answered.

136

"Was she dull?" asked my lord.

"I do not think so," I said.

"Then why," he went on, "did she change a way of life which was so convenient and agreeable for one which is tiresome and insipid? It appears to me——"

"It appears to me," interrupted his relative, "that Miss Cecilia might have three reasons, that is to say any one of three reasons, any of which would do her credit."

"And what might these reasons be?" asked the young man.

"Firstly she may have feared that the world might censure the manner of living which we are regretting, and that women, vexed at no longer having these two ladies amongst them, and envying them the attentions of all the men who visited them, might make unjust or unkind remarks; now a woman, and how much more a young girl, cannot be at too great pains to avoid idle talk or anything that gives rise to it."

"And your second reason? Let me see," said my lord, "if I think it any better than your first."

"Miss Cecilia may have inspired in someone who visits here a sentiment to which she does not feel inclined to respond, and which, in consequence, she does not wish to encourage."

"And the third?"

"It is not impossible that she herself may have felt the commencement of a preference to which she does not wish to abandon herself."

"Men will be grateful to you for the first and last conjectures," said my lord. "It is a pity that they are so gratuitous and that we have so little reason to believe that we either draw down envy upon these ladies, or cause them to fall in love with us."

"But my lord," said his cousin, smiling, "as you insist that one should be as modest for you as for oneself, allow me to inform you that two gentlemen come here who are perhaps more amiable than either of us."

"Here is Miss Cecilia!" said my lord. "I do not believe you would care for me to give her an account of your conjectures, however honourable you may think them."

"Just as you please," was the reply.

Cecilia came in. Her eyes sparkled with pleasure.

"Let us have a modest game of chess again without anyone to interfere," suggested my lord.

"I should like it," said Cecilia, "but it is not possible. In a quarter of an hour I must go and dress my hair and myself for the assembly at Madame de X——'s (she is the wife of our relative, to whose house we had been asked), and I should prefer to talk for a few moments than to play half a game of chess."

And she began to converse in a manner so quiet, so thoughtful, and so serious that I thought I had never seen her so amiable. The two Englishmen waited while she was making her toilet. She came back simply and elegantly dressed and, after we had all admired her a little, we went out. At the door of the house to which we were bound my lord's cousin said that they had better not enter with us and that he wished first to pay another visit.

" Would they then envy these ladies," my lord enquired, " the privilege of being escorted by us? "

" No," said his cousin, " but they might envy *us* our privilege of escorting them and I wish to cause chagrin to no one."

We entered, my daughter and I. The assembly was large; Madame de X—— had expended much care on a head-dress that was meant to appear negligent. Her husband did not stay long in the saloon, and he was no longer there when two young Frenchmen were introduced, one of whom looked exceedingly lively, the other vastly serious. I did nothing but run into the first; he appeared to be everywhere at once, but the other remained immovable in the place where chance first placed him. Then our Englishmen came in. They asked Madame de X—— where her husband was. " Ask mademoiselle," she said in a tone of mockery, pointing to my daughter; " he spoke only to her, and then, content with having had that happiness, he went away immediately. Thereupon the Englishmen went up to Cecilia, and she said, without showing any discomfiture, that her cousin had complained of a severe headache and had proposed to General d'A—— to play a game of piquet in an ante-room removed from the noise. I then quitted Cecilia with perfect confidence, and went to ask my cousin if he indeed had so bad a headache as she supposed, or if he had found his situation in the saloon embarrassing.

"Are you barbarous enough to laugh at me?" he asked (I must tell you, by the by, that the worthy General d'A—— is a little deaf); "but, never mind, I will make my confession. I *did* have a headache, my health has never recovered from this wound (he showed me his hand); that, however, would not have compelled me to withdraw, but I felt that I should be excessively embarrassed; and then I have always found men terribly awkward in their own houses in large assemblies and I had the vanity not to wish you to watch me flitting foolishly from woman to woman, from table to table. This kind of assembly being, on the contrary, the triumph of the mistress of the house, I wished Madame de X—— to enjoy all her advantages without running the risk of spoiling her pleasure by putting her out of humour."

I was making fun of all this nicety when one of the Frenchmen came and put his head into the room. He opened the door completely as soon as he saw me.

"I wager, madam," he said, bowing to me, "that you are the sister, the aunt, or the mother of a pretty person whom I have just seen in there."

"Which pretty person?" I asked.

"Ah, you know very well, madam," he answered.

I said: "Well, I am her mother, but how did you guess it?"

"It was not by her features," he said, "but by her expression and countenance; but how can you leave her a prey to the avenging fury of the mistress of the house? I implored her not to drink a cup of tea that was handed her and to say that she had seen a spider fall into it; but mademoiselle your daughter shrugged her shoulders and drank. She is courageous, or else she, like Alexander, has faith in virtue; but for my part I have more belief in the jealousy of Madame de X——. Mademoiselle has certainly robbed her of her husband or her lover; but I think it must be her husband, for the lady looks rather vain than tender. I should like to see the gentleman. I am sure that he is very amiable and very much in love. Besides, I have heard here, and in the town where his regiment was garrisoned, that he was the most amiable as well as the bravest cavalier in the world. But that, madam, is not the only interesting situation that mademoiselle your daughter is giving spectators the opportunity of admiring. She has at her side two Bernese gentlemen, one German, and an English lord, who is the only one to whom she does not pay much heed. He appears to be distressed at this. But he is not very clever, in my opinion. I think that in his place I should rather be flattered. That distinction is as good as another."

"Your pictures appear to me to be imaginary," I said to him, smiling, but I was in truth much distressed. "Let us go and see."

I shut the door of the ante-room after leaving it.

"Do you know, monsieur," I said, "that you were speaking before the master of the house? It was he who was playing."

He promptly opened the door again, and took me back to the piquet players. "What, monsieur," he said to my relative, "can a young madcap say to a gallant gentleman who pretended not to hear the nonsense that he was talking?"

"Just what you are saying, monsieur," replied Monsieur de X——, rising. And cordially pressing the hand that the young stranger extended, he put forward a chair and bade us both be seated. He then enquired for news of several officers of his regiment and of other persons whom the young man had recently seen. I, in my turn, questioned him, asking him what his brother was.

"An officer of the artillery," he said, "full of talent and industry, but nothing more than that."

"And you yourself?" I said.

"A scatterbrain—a wag, and I, also, nothing more than that. I believed, in truth, that that profession would satisfy me until I was twenty; but I am only seventeen and should like to relinquish it already. Indeed, it would be too late, by one day."

"And what profession do you propose to adopt in its place?"

"I always swore to myself," he answered, "to be a hero when I ceased to be a madcap. When I am twenty I intend to be a hero. I should like to employ the interval of three years in preparing myself for that trade, better than I should be able to do if I did not desert my present one."

"Thank you," I said. "I am perfectly satisfied with you and your answers. Let us now go and see what my daughter is doing. I must bid the apprentice hero to remember that prudence, loyalty, and discretion about ladies formed part of the profession of his most celebrated precursors, those of whom the troubadours of his country sung the love and the deeds. I must beg him not to say a word of my daughter which is not worthy of the most discreet and gallant cavalier."

"I promise it you, not in jest but in earnest," he replied. "It would not be possible for me to keep silence too scrupulously after the imprudence with which I have already spoken."

We were by then in the saloon. My daughter was playing whist with some boys, princes, it is true, but none the less the most ill-licked cubs in the world.

"Look!" said my Frenchman, "the English lord, and the handsome Bernese have been placed at the other end of the room."

"No comments!" I replied.

"May I be permitted to show you my brother who, seated in the same place as when we left him, is still bombarding and cannonading the same town; Gibraltar perhaps? This table is the fortress, or perhaps it is Maestricht which he has to defend."

His chatter would never have ceased if I had not

asked to be allowed to play.   I was about to finish my game when my cousin came back to the saloon. He came up to me.

" Can it be," he asked, " that this young rattle saw in a moment that which I had not yet seen with all my anxiety?   Can it be that he has come to remove from me an uncertainty of which I now appreciate the value? "

He sat down sadly beside me, not daring to approach my daughter, nor able to compel himself to approach his wife or my lord.

" I shall let you think so," I said.   " You would only otherwise transfer your suspicions to some-one else and that might cause you even more distress, for this boy does not seem to me to be very distinguished either in mind or in countenance. However, ask yourself if it is very reasonable to put so much faith in the observations that a young madcap has been able to make in a quarter of an hour? "

" That madcap," he said, " understood my wife."

We withdrew: I left my cousin plunged in gloom.   Our Englishmen escorted us home and my lord begged with so much urgency to be permitted to sup with us that I had not the heart to refuse.   They told me about all the cutting remarks, the unfriendly glances of our hostess. They spoke of the game in which she was com-pelled to join.   Cecilia said nothing, but, drawing me aside, " Do not let us complain, mamma," she

144

murmured, " and do not let us laugh at her; in her place I should perhaps act likewise."

" Not," I replied, " like her, from self-love."

Our supper was gay. The young lord appeared to be enchanted at not having any Bernese, any Frenchmen, any competitors round him. On taking leave he told me that this time he would adopt the tactics of his governor and say nothing about the supper, for fear of attracting envy. I should not have requested secrecy of him but am not sorry that he should observe it. My cousin causes me to feel real pity for him. The young Frenchmen go away to-morrow. They have produced a great sensation here; but in admiring the intelligence and the application of the elder brother people regretted that he did not talk a little more; and, in admiring the vivacity of mind and the charm of the younger, they wished that he had talked a little less, and had been prudent and modest, without reflecting that in that case there would have been nothing either to admire or to criticize in either of them. People do not sufficiently realize that, with us poor mortals, the reverse of the medal is of its essence, quite as much as the right side. Change one thing, and you change everything. In the perfect mean you find mediocrity as well as wisdom.

Farewell! I am sending you, by your husband's relatives, the portrait of Cecilia.

LETTER XVI

(The same)

I am going to copy for you a letter from Cecilia's
Bernese suitor, which my cousin the soldier has
just sent me. It is as follows:

"Your relative, Cecilia de C——, is the first
woman whom I have desired to call mine. She
and her mother are the first women with whom
I have been able to think I should be happy to
pass my life. Tell me, my dear friend, you who
really know them, if I am mistaken in the completely favourable opinion that I have formed of
them. Tell me also (for this is another question),
tell me, without feeling obliged to state your
reasons, in particular whether you advise me to
attach myself to Cecilia and to ask her mother for
her hand."

Beneath this my cousin had written in answer:
"To your first question I answer 'yes' without
hesitation; and yet I answer 'no' to the second.
If that which causes me to say 'no' changes, or if
my opinion in this respect changes, I will let you
know immediately."

To me he wrote under the same cover: "Have
the obligingness, madam, to let me know if you
and Mademoiselle Cecilia approve my reply. If
you do not approve it I will not send it, but will
make instead any reply that you dictate."

Cecilia had gone out and I awaited her return to

146

give my answer. She approved my cousin's reply. I said to her, " Think well, dear child."

" I *have* thought," she answered.

" Do not be vexed with my question," I said. " Do you think your Englishman more amiable? "

She said she did not.

" Do you think him more honest, more tender, or gentler? "

" No."

" Do you find him more elegant in his person? "

" No."

" You would live, at least in summer, in the Pays-de-Vaud. Would you prefer to live in an unknown country? "

" I should a hundred times rather live here and I should rather live in Berne than in London."

" Would it be indifferent to you to enter a family where you would not be seen with approbation? "

" No; that would appear to me very uncomfortable."

" Have you come to some mutual understanding or expressed some mutual sympathy; is it that, dear child? "

" No, mamma. I only occupy my lord's mind at most when he sees me, and I do not believe that he truly prefers me to his horse, his new boots, or his English whip."

She smiled sadly, and two tears glistened in her eyes.

" Does it not seem possible to you, dear child, to forget such a lover? " I asked her.

" It seems possible; but I do not know if it will happen."

" Are you sure that you would be happy un-married? "

" I am *not* sure, that is again one of those things that one cannot know beforehand."

" And yet your cousin's reply? "

" His reply is correct, mamma, and I beg you to write to our cousin and request him to send it."

" Far better write yourself," I said.   She folded an envelope for the letter and wrote.

" Your reply is correct, monsieur, and I thank you for it.
" CECILIA DE C———."

The letter despatched, my daughter handed me my work and took up hers.

" You asked me, mamma," she said, " if I should be happy unmarried.   It seems to me that that would depend entirely on the kind of life that I was able to lead.   I have already often thought that if I had nothing to do but to be a spinster among folk who had husbands, wives, mistresses, lovers, and children I might find it very sad and might covet sometimes, as you said the other day, the husband or the lover of my neigh-bour; but if you were willing to go to Holland or to England to keep a shop or to open a pension,

I believe that, being always busy and in your company, and not having the time either to go into society or to read romances, I should envy and regret nothing, and that my life might be very sweet. Hope would supply what was lacking in reality. I should flatter myself with the belief of becoming one day sufficiently rich to buy a house surrounded with a meadow, an orchard, and a garden somewhere between Lausanne and Rolle, or perhaps between Vevey and Villeneuve, and of passing the rest of my life with you there."

" That would be all very well," I corrected, " if we had chanced to be twin sisters; but I thank you, Cecilia, for your project pleases and touches me. If it were more rational it would perhaps touch me less."

" People die at all ages," she said, " and perhaps you will have the tedium of surviving me."

" Yes," I replied, " but there *is* an age when one cannot live any longer and that age will come for me nineteen years sooner than for you. . . . "

Our words ceased then, but not our reflections. Six o'clock had struck and we went out, for we do not now pass our evenings at home unless we really have company here, that is to say, women as well as men. I have never gone out so little as during last month and never so much as during this one. Solitude is a matter of chance and taste: dissipation is a painful task. If I were not during half the time very uneasy in society, I should be fatigued to death. Every respite from anxiety is filled with tedium. Sometimes I rest and recreate myself by taking a little walk with my daughter, or even, as to-day, by sitting alone opposite an open window which looks out over the lake. I thank you, mountains, snow, and sunshine, for all the happiness that you give me. I thank you, Author of all that I see, for having willed that these things should be so agreeable to contemplate. Oh striking and admirable beauties of nature, every day my eyes admire you, every day you make yourselves felt in my heart! . . .

LETTER XVII

(The same)

My dear friend, you have given me even more pleasure than you anticipated by saying that the silhouette of Cecilia pleased you so much, and that the stories of the Chevalier de X—— had made you very curious to see both mother and daughter. Very good; it only depends on you to enjoy the felicity. My daughter is losing her gaiety through the restraint that she has imposed on herself. If that continued much longer I should fear her losing her freshness, even perhaps her health. During some days past I have been reflecting how to avert a misfortune which is terrible to me even in imagination, and which would be intolerable in reality. When congratulated on her good manners or praised for her education I could not help feeling a desire to cry which could not always be suppressed, and I passed all the time that I was alone in imagining some way of distracting my daughter, of giving her back happiness, and of preserving her health and her life. (For my fears in truth know no bounds.) But I found no plan that satisfied me.

It is too early in the season to go to the country. If I hired a country place at this season and went there, what gossip would it not give rise to? And even later, if I hired one close to Lausanne, besides being very dear, it would not have provided adequate change of scene; and, farther off, in our mountains or in the valley of the Lac de Joux, my daughter, being no longer in the public eye, would have been exposed to the most unjust and injurious conjectures. Then your letter came and all uncertainty was at an end. I told my plan to my daughter. She accepted it courageously. We shall therefore visit you, unless you forbid us; but I am so sure that you will not forbid us that I shall immediately announce our departure and let my house to some strangers who are looking for one. I need not be distressed on my cousin's account, for he himself will be relieved at our departure, and I am very glad on account of the young Bernese gentleman. If my lord permits us to leave without declaring himself, or if, at any rate, after our departure, when he realizes what he has lost, he does not pursue us, does not write, does not beg of his parents the permission to present Cecilia to them as a daughter, I flatter myself that she will forget a youth so little worthy of her tenderness, and that she will render justice to a man superior to him in every respect.

LETTER XVIII

(The same)

We are awaiting your reply in a pretty house that has been lent us, three quarters of a league from Lausanne. The foreigners who had desired to take mine, and who did take it, were in haste to assume possession. I left them all my furniture, so that we had neither fatigue nor trouble. It is possible that if the snow does not melt, or does not melt altogether, we may not be able to leave as soon as we desired. That is now somewhat indifferent to me, but when we left Lausanne I should rather have had farther to go and fresher scenes to offer to the eyes and the imagination of my daughter; for whatever tenderness a girl may feel for her mother, it seemed to me that to find herself alone with her in the month of March might appear a little melancholy. It would have been the first time that I had seen Cecilia dull in my company or desirous that our tête-à-tête should be interrupted. I admit to you that, from an apprehension of this mortification, I did all in

152

my power to avert it. A portfolio of prints that Monsieur d'Ey had lent us, the " Thousand and One Nights," the " Contes " of Hamilton, " Gil Blas," and " Zadig " had preceded us, together with a pianoforte and a supply of needlework. Other things not due to my thoughtfulness have perhaps done more—my lord, his relative, a wretched dog, a poor negro. . . . But I will take up my narrative from farther back.

After writing to you, I arranged to go to a rout where I knew that I should find all the fine folk of Lausanne. I advised Cecilia not to come till half an hour later, after I had announced that my house was to be let, and had published our departure; but she said that she was interested in seeing the impression I should make.

" You *will* see it," I said, " my plan would only save you the first astonishment and the first interrogations."

" No, mamma," she said, " let me be witness to the whole impression, that I may have all the pleasure or all the chagrin. At your side, leaning against your chair, touching your arm or even only your gown, I shall feel myself confident in the most powerful as well as the most amiable protection. You well know, mamma, how much you love *me*, but not how much I love *you*, and how, having you, I could support the loss or the renunciation of everything besides. Let me go, mamma, you are too timid, and conceive me weaker than I am."

Is it needful to tell you, my friend, that I

embraced Cecilia, that I pressed her to my heart, that I wept; that, in walking in the street I leaned upon her arm with more than common joy and tenderness, that, on entering the room, I was careful immediately to have a chair for her placed a little behind mine? Oh, you doubtless *can* imagine all that; but can you picture my poor cousin and his friend the English governor coming to us with troubled looks, seeking in our eyes an explanation for what they saw that was novel and strange? My cousin, in particular, looked at me, then at Cecilia, and appeared equally to desire and to dread my speaking; and the Englishman, who saw this agitation, divided his interest between him and us, now passing his arm absently round Monsieur X——, now putting his hand on his shoulder, as if to say: "At last I have really become your friend; if you hear anything vexatious you will find a true friend in the foreigner in whom you have only found till now sympathy, and a certain affinity in character or circumstance." I, myself, who all day had only been considering your letter and my reply in relation to my daughter, and had been thinking only about her and her impressions, I was so much moved by what I perceived of the passion of one of these men and the tenderness of the other, by the habits and affection that united them and us, and the sort of farewell that it was now necessary to bid them, that I began to weep. Imagine their perplexity and my daughter's surprise!

The silence became insupportable; the uneasiness increased, my cousin grew pale, Cecilia pressed my arm and whispered to me, " But, mamma, what is it? what is the matter with you? "

" I am quite mad," I said to them at laſt. " What is it all about? A journey which is neither likely to take us out of the world, nor even to the other end of it. Languedoc is no great diſtance. You, sir, you are yourself travelling, and we may hope to meet you again; and you, my cousin, are going in the same direction as ourselves. We wish to visit my amiable relative who is a very agreeable woman and exceedingly dear to me. She, too, desires to see us; there is no obſtacle, and I am determined to ſtart very soon. Go, my cousin, and inform Monsieur and Madame B—— that my house is to be let for six months."

He departed on this errand; and meanwhile the Englishman took a chair beside us. Very soon my daughter's guardians and their wives rushed up; my lord, seeing us occupied in conversing with them, leaned againſt the chimney-piece, looking far away. The young Bernese came to express his pleasure at spending the summer nearer to us than he had expected. Then the foreigners I had heard of came in, and immediately offered to hire my house. Nothing remained but the difficulty of lodging ourselves while awaiting your reply. We were offered an apartment in a country house that an English family had quitted laſt autumn. I accepted this offer with eagerness, so that everything was settled and made public in a quarter of an hour; but the astonishment, the exclamations, lasted all the evening. Those who were the most interested in our departure spoke the least about it. My lord contented himself with learning the distance from Lausanne to the dwelling that had been lent us, and with assuring us that the road to Lyons would not be practicable for ladies for a long time; he then asked his governor if, instead of commencing their tour of France by Berne, Basle, Strasbourg, Nancy, Metz, Paris, they could not commence by Lyons, Marseilles, Toulouse. . . .

" Would you then find it more easy to quit Toulouse than now to stay away from it? " was the reply.

" I cannot tell," said my lord, more feebly and with less significance than I could have desired.

" After having been six weeks in Paris," said his relative, " you shall go wherever you like."

Cecilia begged me to let her help to play my hand, saying that her head was so full of our journey that our own play would be worthless. After the game she asked Monsieur d'Ey to lend us some engravings and books; my cousin offered his pianoforte, which I accepted, his wife being no musician. The young Bernese, who has his chaise and horses here, begged me to make use of them to carry us to the country, and to permit his coachman to enquire each morning of a milkmaid, who goes to town, whether I could employ him during the day.

" No; I, myself," said my lord, " whenever the weather is tolerable, will go to ask if these ladies have any orders, and will convey them to you."

" That is as it should be," said his relative, " we poor strangers have only our zeal to offer."

Madame de X——, my cousin's wife, seeing everyone clustered round us, approached at length and said to her husband: " And you, sir, as these ladies are leaving, will perhaps at last be prevailed upon to make up your mind to go also; you will perhaps no longer have letters to write every day, or excuses to offer. For a whole week," she added, affecting to laugh, " have his trunks been fastened to his carriage." Everyone kept silence. " But seriously, sir," she went on, " when are you leaving? "

" To-morrow, madam, or this evening," he replied, growing very pale. And, hurrying to the door, after having pressed his friend's hand, he left the room and the house. Indeed, he left Lausanne that same night, his road illumined by moonlight and the snow.

The following day, which was Monday, and the day after, I was busy and could see no one, and last Wednesday, by midday, we, that is Cecilia, Fanchon, Philax, and I, were in our carriage on the road to Rennes. Orders had, of course, been given to open our apartment and to light a fire in the dining-room, and we were expecting to make our dinner off a milk soup and some eggs. But, on approaching the house, we were surprised to see an air of movement and animation, all the windows open, and in all the rooms huge fires, which competed with the sunshine in drying and warming the air and the furniture. When we reached the door my lord and his governor assisted us to descend from the chaise and carried our packages and boxes into the house. The table was laid, the pianoforte tuned, and a favourite air open on its desk, a cushion for the dog was by the fire, flowers in the vases on the mantelpiece; nothing could have been more gallant or more elegantly contrived. An excellent dinner was served; we drank punch; they left us some provisions, a pasty, lemons, some rum, and they begged to be allowed to come and dine with us once or twice in every week.

"As to drinking tea with you, madam," said my lord, "I do not even ask permission for *that*; you would refuse it to no one."

At five o'clock their horses were brought, and as the weather was fine, although very cold, we accompanied them as far as the high road. At the moment when we were about to separate, there came running up to us a fine dog, a great Dane, rubbing his muzzle along the snow-covered ground; it was his last effort, he looked about him as if bewildered, trembled, and fell at Cecilia's feet. She bent down. My lord cried out and attempted to stop her, but Cecilia, insisting that the dog was not mad but had only lost its master and was half dead with fatigue, cold, and fear, went on caressing him. The lackeys were sent back to the house to fetch bread, milk, whatever they could find. The food was brought; the dog ate and drank and licked the hands of his benefactress. Cecilia wept with joy and pity. Absorbed by suiting her pace to that of the tired animal, as she took it home, she had scarcely a glance for her departing lover, and all the evening she was occupied in warming and consoling this new friend, in finding a name for him, in conjecturing the cause of his misfortune, in anticipating the chagrin and jealousy of Philax. And on retiring she made a bed of all her clothes for the unfortunate dog, so that he became in truth the most fortunate dog in the world.

That was Wednesday; we were settled in our retreat, and Cecilia did not appear at all likely to be dull; she had not yet had recourse to half her distractions; books, prints, needlework, all yet remaining in a drawer.

Thursday came; flowers, the dog, the piano sufficed for the morning. In the afternoon Cecilia went to visit the farmer who occupied part of the house; she caressed his children, conversed with his wife and, on seeing them take some milk from the kitchen, she learned that they were carrying it to a sick man, a negro, who was dying of consumption, and whom the English family whom he had served had left in the house. They had recommended him warmly to the kindness of the farmer and his wife, and had given a banker in Lausanne an order to pay them every week, so long as he lived, a pension more than sufficient to enable them to take good care of him. Cecilia came back to tell me all this and to beg me to go with her to the negro and to speak English to him, so as to find out if we could procure him anything that he lacked.

"They tell me, mamma," she said, "that he knows no French, and perhaps these people, for all their good will, cannot divine his wishes."

We went to him, and Cecilia spoke to him the first words of English that she had ever uttered. The negro seemed to hear her with pleasure. He was not suffering, but there was hardly any life left in him. Gentle, patient, and tranquil he nourished neither wishes nor regrets; and yet he was still young. Cecilia and Fanchon scarcely left him. They gave him from time to time a little wine or a little soup. I myself was seated beside him with Cecilia when, on Sunday morning, he died. We remained motionless for a time.

"So *that* is how we end, mamma," said Cecilia, "how that which feels and speaks and moves ceases to feel, to hear, and to move! What a strange fate he had! To be born in Guinea, to be sold into slavery, to cultivate sugar in Jamaica, to serve in an English family, and to die in Lausanne! Poor man! Yet why should I say 'poor man'? Whether a man dies in his own country or in another, whether he lives a longer or shorter time, whether he has a little more or a little less pleasure or pain, still the moment comes when all are equal; the king of France will, some day, be like this negro."

" And I, also," I interrupted, " and you . . . and my lord."

" Yes," she said, " that is quite true; but now let us leave this place. I see Fanchon coming back from church and I must tell her."

She went to meet Fanchon, and embraced her, and wept, and came back to fondle her dogs and to continue weeping. To-day the negro is to be buried. This time we have truly seen death as it really is, with nothing added; nothing awful, nothing solemn, nothing pathetic. No relatives, no mourning, no lamentations, affected or real; and as a consequence, my daughter has received no lugubrious impression. She returned to the dead man two or three times each day; she insisted on having him left in his own bed, covered and un- touched, and in having the room warmed. She even read and worked in the room and she ended by making me as reasonable as herself.

* * * * *

LETTER XIX

(From Mme. de C. to Mr. William D.)

SIR,

You appeared yesterday to be so sad that I feel constrained to enquire the cause of your grief. You will perhaps refuse to tell it me, but you cannot be affronted at my enquiry. My lord comes to see us almost every day. It is true that he usually stays only for a moment. Do you blame me for receiving him? You know him as well as a young man can be known; you know his parents, and their views about him. I do not doubt that you have read into my daughter's heart. Tell me what I ought to do. I am, sir, your very humble and obedient servant,

C. DE C.

LETTER XX

(Mr. W. D. to Mme. de C.)

MADAM,

It is quite true that I am exceedingly unhappy. I am so far from being offended by your enquiry that I had already resolved to tell you my story; now, instead, I shall write it. It will be a kind of occupation and a distraction, indeed the only one of which I am at present capable.

All that I can tell you, madam, about my lord, is that I know of no vice in him. I do not know if he loves Mademoiselle Cecilia as much as she deserves; but I am almost sure that he regards no other woman with interest and has no other attachment of any kind. Two months ago I wrote to his father that the young man appeared to be attaching himself to a girl without fortune, but whose birth, breeding, character, and countenance left nothing to be desired, and I asked him if he wished me to make use of some pretext to remove him from Lausanne; for to have attempted to separate him from you and your daughter here, madam, would have been to as much as have said to him that there were merits superior to beauty, goodness, dignity, and wit. I had better reason even than most men for not undertaking so odious and ridiculous a task. His father and mother replied that, so long as their son loved and was beloved, and married from love and not from reasons of honour, when love had passed, they would be satisfied, and that, from the manner in which I spoke of the young lady to whom he was attached and of her mother, there appeared no reason for apprehension. They were doubtless quite in the right; nevertheless I depicted to the young man himself the shame, the despair he would feel if he saw himself obliged to fulfil, in cold blood, an engagement that he had undertaken in a moment of intoxication; for to fail in such an engagement I did not desire him to believe possible.

I do not think, madam, that his visits will be considered strange. He had announced them previous to your departure and before everyone. He is observed every day occupied with his studies and almost every evening in the company of other ladies. I have received news of your relative from Lyons; nothing disagreeable happened to him in spite of his having travelled day and night and the roads being more deeply covered with snow than they have ever before been at this season. He is not happy.

I shall possibly commence my narration this evening.

I have the honour to be, madam, etc., etc.

WILLIAM D.

END OF THE FIRST PART

LETTERS FROM LAUSANNE

2nd Series

" CALISTE "

CALISTE

(From Mr. W. D. to Mme. de C.)

M Y STORY, MADAM, IS AS ROMANTIC AS IT IS melancholy, and you will be disagreeably surprised to discover that circumstances, so extraordinary as to be scarcely credible, have produced only a very ordinary man.

My brother and I were born almost at the same hour, and our birth occasioned the death of our mother. My father's extreme distress, together with the commotion that reigned for a few moments in the whole house, caused the two infants who had just been born to be confounded. It was never known which of us was the elder. One of our relatives always thought it to be my brother but without being sure of it; and her evidence, being neither supported nor contradicted by anyone else, produced a sort of presumption, but nothing more; for the belief that had been conceived crumbled whenever its foundations came to be examined. It made a slight impression on *my* mind, but exercised no influence over that of my brother. He made a vow to own nothing except in common with me; and not to marry if I should do so. I made a similar vow, in order to ensure our having but one family between the two of us and therefore only the same heirs, so that the law should never be compelled to decide between our rights or our claims.

Fate, in having thus established between us all the equality possible, had merely imitated Nature; education served but to strengthen and establish this conformity. We resembled each other in appearance and temper, our tastes were the same, our employments as well as our diversions were shared; one of us did nothing without the other, and the friendship between us was more of our essence than our choice, so that we were scarcely aware of it. Others indeed remarked it; we ourselves only realized it fully when there came a thought of separating us. My brother was destined for a place in Parliament and I to serve in the Army; it was designed to send him to Oxford and to place me with an engineer; but when the moment of separation came, our distress and our prayers caused me to be permitted to follow him to the University, and I shared all his studies, and he all mine. I learned law and history with him, and he mathematics and tactics with me; while we were equal in our devotion to literature and the fine arts. It was at this period that we began to appreciate the strength of the feeling that united us; and if this understanding did not render our friendship the more complete or tender, it did make it more productive of action, sentiment, and thought; so that, being more conscious of it, we enjoyed it the more. Castor and Pollux, Orestes and Pylades, Achilles and Patrocles, Nessus and Euryalus, David and Jonathan were our heroes.

We persuaded ourselves that, if a man had a
friend, he could be neither cowardly nor vicious,
for the fault of the one friend would reflect on the
other and each would have to blush, to suffer, for
the other's fault. Moreover, what motive could
induce in either of us a wicked action? Sure of
each other, what wealth, what ambition, what
mistress, could afford sufficient temptation for
offence? In history, in mythology, everywhere,
we sought for instances of friendship; and that
virtue appeared to us to contain in itself all virtue
and all felicity.

Three years passed; the war in America broke
out and the regiment of which I had now long
worn the uniform received its marching orders.
My brother came to inform me of this, and, in
speaking of the departure and the voyage, I was
surprised to hear him say " we " instead of " you."
I stared at him.

" Did you imagine that I should permit you to
start alone? " he said. And, seeing that I wished
to speak, " Do not make any objection," he cried,
" it would be the first sorrow that you had ever
caused me."

He went to pass a few days with my father, who,
together with all our relatives, urged my brother
to abandon his strange project. But he remained
unmoved, and we set off together. The first
campaign held nothing that was not pleasing and
honourable. A sub-lieutenant of the company in

which I had the honour to serve having been killed, my brother solicited and obtained his place. Dressed alike, of the same figure, having almost similar hair and features, people confused us incessantly, in spite of seeing us continually side by side. During the winter we found means to continue our studies, to elevate plans, to draw maps, to play the harp, the lute, and the violin, while our comrades wasted their time with women and play. I do not blame them; company and occupation are necessary to man.

At the beginning of the second campaign. . . . But of what use is it to detail to you that which brought upon me the most terrible of all misfortunes? He was wounded at my side. " Poor William! " he said as he was carried off, " what will become of you? " For three days I lived between hope and fear; during three days I was witness of the most atrocious suffering most patiently borne. At length, on the evening of the third day, seeing him grow worse from moment to moment, I cried, " Perform a miracle, O God, and give him back to me."

" Nay, deign rather to comfort my brother," murmured the dying man in tones that were scarcely audible. He then pressed my hand feebly and expired.

I do not recollect clearly what occurred in the time immediately subsequent to my brother's death. I found myself back in England; I was taken to Bristol and to Bath. I seemed a wandering

ghost, a poor, useless shadow of my former self.
One day at Bath I was seated on one of the seats
upon the promenade, sometimes turning the pages
of a book that I had brought with me, sometimes
letting it lie idle beside me. A lady whom I
remembered to have seen before came and seated
herself at the other end of the bench; we remained
long without speaking, I scarcely observing her;
at length I turned my eyes towards her and
answered some questions that she put me in her
low and modest voice. I thought it was only
through motives of politeness and gratitude that I
escorted her to her home a few minutes later; but
the next day and the following days I sought to see
her again; and her gentle conversation and soft
attentions caused me soon to prefer her company
to my own sad reveries, which, until then, had
been my only resource.

Caliste (for that was the name which remained to
her from the part which she had played with the
greatest success on the first and only occasion of
her appearance on the stage), Caliste was of
respectable birth and connected with a family of
fortune; but a vicious mother who had sunk into
poverty, wishing to draw profit from her daughter's face, her talents, and her exquisite voice, had
destined her from infancy to the theatre, and the
girl had made her *début* as " Caliste " in *The Fair
Penitent*. At the close of the performance a gentleman of position went to ask her of her mother,
purchased her, one might indeed say, and, the

following morning, left with her for the continent. She was placed in Paris in a famous convent, under the name of " Caliste," and was held to be a girl of noble birth, whose family name had to be concealed for reasons of discretion.

She was adored by the nuns and by her companions; and the tone that she might have caught from her mother betrayed her so little that she was thought to be the daughter of the late Duke of Cumberland, and cousin, consequently, of our King. When this supposition was spoken of to her the blushes, occasioned by her knowledge of her true situation, fortified the suspicion, rather than destroyed it. She was soon able to perform with astonishing address all the accomplishments of a young lady. She began to draw and to paint, she had already danced sufficiently well for her mother to have thought of making her a dancer; and now she perfected herself in this seductive art; she also took lessons in singing and on the harpsichord. I always thought that she played and sang as one speaks or ought to speak, and as she herself did speak; I mean that she sang and played sometimes from improvisation, sometimes from memory anything that was asked of her, anything that was given her, letting herself be interrupted and beginning again a hundred times, seldom considering her own preferences, and, above all, delighting in making others shine. But this degree of perfection and facility she did not acquire in Paris, but in Italy, where her lover passed two years alone with her, completely absorbed in her company, her development, and her happiness. After four years of travel he brought her back to England, and, living with her, sometimes at his country place, sometimes with his uncle, General D——, he enjoyed four more years of life and felicity. But happiness and love do not vanquish death, and he fell a victim to an inflamation of the lungs.

"I leave her nothing," he said to his uncle a moment before he died, "because I now possess nothing; but *you* are still living and are wealthy. What she has from you will be more honourable than anything that I could give her. In this respect I regret nothing, and I die tranquil."

This uncle gave Caliste, together with an income of £400, the house at Bath where I found her established. He came there himself for a few weeks each year, and whenever he had the gout he caused her to visit him.

She resembles you, madam, or she *resembled* you—I do not know which expression to employ! In her thoughts, in her judgments, in her manners, she had, like you, a manner of passing over small considerations in order to go straight to the root of the matter, to that which is really important in people and things. Her soul and her speech, her tone and her thought, were always in accord; that which was only ingenious did not interest her prudence in itself never determined her, and she said that she did not really know what reason was.

But she grew ingenious in order to oblige others, and prudent to spare them distress, and she appeared to be reason itself when she desired to soften painful memories and to bring back calm to a tormented heart and mind. You, madam, are sometimes gay and often impulsive; she was never either the one or the other. Dependent, although adored, despised by some while she was served upon their knees by others, she had contracted a melancholy reserve that had something in it of both pride and fear. If she had been less loving she might have appeared bashful and unapproachable. One day, on seeing her withdraw herself from some strangers who had approached her with assiduity and were regarding her with admiration, I asked her what were her motives in acting thus.

"Let us go near them," she said, " they have enquired my name, you will see how they *now* will look at me!" We made the experiment; she had divined only too truly, and a tear accompanied the smiling glance with which she made me observe it.

"What does it matter to you?" I asked her.

"One day it *may* matter to me," she said, her colour rising. I only understood her a long time afterwards.

I remember that, another time, when invited by a lady to whose house I was going, she refused.

"But why?" I asked her. " This woman, and

all those whom you will see at her house, are intelligent people who will honour you."

" Ah," she said, " it is not marked contempt that I most dread; I know my own heart and that of those who despise me too well to put myself at their level; no; it is complaisance, the care taken not to mention actresses or kept women or to speak of my lord or of his uncle that I fear. When I see kindness and goodness made uneasy on my account and obliged to restrain or falsify themselves, I myself suffer. During my lord's lifetime gratitude rendered me more sociable; I endeavoured to win the hearts of others so that his might not be wounded. If his servants had not respected me, if his relatives or friends had repulsed me, or if I had avoided them, he would have broken with everyone. Those who went to his house were so much accustomed to me that often, without thinking, they said before me the most offensive things. A thousand times I have smilingly signed to my lord to let them talk; sometimes I was indeed glad that they *should* forget what manner of woman I was, sometimes I was flattered that they should regard me as an exception to others of my kind; and indeed what was said of such women's effrontery, arts, and avarice, had certainly nothing to do with me."

" Why did he not marry you? " I asked.

" He only spoke once of it to me," she answered. " Then he said, ' Marriage between us would only be an empty ceremony which would add nothing

either to my respect for you or to the inviolable
attachment that I have sworn to you; nevertheless, if I had a throne to give you or even a passable
fortune, I should not hesitate; but I am almost
ruined, you are far younger than I am; of what
service would it be to you to leave you a title
without a fortune? Either I know my public ill,
or the lady who has gained nothing by being my
companion but the pleasure of making the man
who adored her the happiest of men, will be more
respected than one to whom a title and a rank
were bequeathed.' " [1]

You will be surprised, perhaps, madam, at the
exactness of my memory, or you may even suspect
me of supplementing and embellishing it. Ah!
when I have completed your acquaintance with her
whose words I retail, you will not think thus, nor
will you be surprised at my recollecting with so
much precision the first conversations that we had
together. For some time back they have indeed
returned to me in astonishing detail; I see the
place where she spoke, and I think to hear her
still. But in order that you should grow to know
her better I must now return to the comparisons
that I have not ceased to make since the first
moment that I had the happiness of meeting you.
More silent than you with those who were
indifferent to her, as loving as you but childless,
she was even more caressing, more attentive, more

[1] Original footnote. " He was mistaken in his world,
and reasoned foolishly."

captivating with her friends. Her wit was not so
bold as yours, but it was neater; her expression
was less vivacious but more tender. In a country
where the fine arts take the place of striking
natural beauty, she had the same sensibility to the
one as you have to the other. Your house is
simple and dignified, it is that of a gentlewoman
who is not rich; hers also was adorned with taste
and economy; she saved all that she could from
her income for the education of penniless girls
whose upbringing she undertook. But she worked
as the fairies do, and every day her friends found
some novelty in her house to admire and to enjoy.
Sometimes it would be a comfortable piece of
furniture that she had herself made; sometimes a
vase, which she herself had designed and which
was to make the workman's fortune. She copied
portraits for her friends, and, for her own pleasure,
the pictures of the best masters. There was no
talent, no art of pleasing that was not in her
power.

Cared for and distracted by her, my health
returned; life no longer appeared to me a burden
too heavy, too worthless to be borne; at last I was
able to weep for my brother and to speak of him
without constraint.

I wept freely, and often I made her weep.

" I see," she said one day, " what has caused you
to be so tender and gentle, and yet so manly.
Most men who have only had ordinary companions
of their own sex have little delicacy or softness,

while those who have lived much among women, although appearing more amiable at first, are less skilful and less hardy in manly exercises, and become in time sedentary, timid, exacting, egotistic, and vapourish, like us. Your excursions, your games and exercises with your brother, rendered you robust and skilful, and your love for him made your naturally sensitive heart soft and tender." " How happy he must have been! " she exclaimed one day when, with my head full of my brother, I had talked long of him; " how happy that woman will be who replaces your beloved brother in your heart! "

" But who will ever love me as he did? " I enquired.

" That would not be difficult," she answered, colouring. " You will never love any woman as you loved him; but if you felt only that tenderness which you still *could* feel, if anyone thought herself the being whom you loved best now that you no longer have your brother. . . ."

I looked at her; tears were streaming from her eyes. I fell at her feet and kissed her hands.

" Did you not see," she asked, " that I loved you? "

" No," I said, " and you are the first woman from whom I have heard those sweet words."

" I am now repaid," she said, " for much reserve, and the sadness of not having my emotions divined. I loved you from the first moment that I saw you; it had been gratitude that had moved

me previously, but never love; I know it now
that it is too late. What a situation is mine! The
less that I deserve to be respected the greater is my
need of respect. I should see only insult in what
to another might be signs of love; humiliated and
frightened at the least breach of decorum I should
remember with horror what I *had* been, what
renders me unworthy of you in my eyes and doubtless in yours, and what I intend never, what I
ought never, to be again. Ah! I have only known
the full value of a flawless life and reputation since
I have known *you*! How often have I not wept
on seeing a girl, even the poorest girl, but one
who was chaste, or at least still innocent. In her
place I should give myself to you, I should devote
my life to you, I should serve you under any name,
any conditions that you desired; I should be
known to you alone; you might marry; I should
serve your wife and children, and I should feel
proud of being so completely your slave, of doing
everything and suffering everything for you. But
I, what can *I* do? What have *I* to offer? Infamous
and degraded I can become neither your equal nor
your servant. You see that I have thought of
everything; my thoughts for so long have been
only of loving you, of the unhappiness and
happiness of loving you. A thousand times I have
wished to save myself from the misfortunes that
I foresee; but who can escape his destiny? At
least in telling you how much I love you I have
given myself one moment of happiness. . . ."

" Let us not foresee misfortunes," I cried, " for my part I foresee nothing; I am with you; and you love me. The present is too delightful for me to torment myself with the future." While speaking I pressed her to my heart. She tore herself free.

" Then I also will not speak of the future," she said, " for I can never endure giving pain to those I love. Go now; leave me to compose myself; and you meanwhile must reflect upon my situation and upon your own; perhaps you will be wiser than I am able to be, and will not entangle yourself in a connection that gives hope of so little felicity. To believe that you will always have it in your power to leave me and not to suffer remorse would be to deceive yourself; but to-day you *could* leave me without cruelty. I should not easily be comforted, but you would have no cause of self-reproach. Your health is recovered; you can leave this place. If you return here to-morrow it will be to tell me that you have accepted the heart I offer you. And then you *can* never, without suffering yourself, make *me* altogether unhappy. Think," she said, pressing my hand, " you are still free, your health is re-established."

" Yes," I said, " but it is to you that I owe it." And I left her.

I was not conscious of reflection or thought or conflict, and yet, as if something were holding me back, I only quitted my house late on the following day. It was thus far advanced in the evening that I found myself at Caliste's door, without being able to say that I had even decided to return there. Heaven! what radiant happiness did I not see in her eyes!

" You have come back; you have come back! " she cried.

" Who," I said, " could have deprived himself of such felicity? After a long night the dawn of happiness begins to break; could I have fled from it and plunged myself back into the gloom of night? "

She looked at me, and, seated opposite me, her hands clasped, weeping and smiling simultaneously, she repeated, " He has come back; he has come back! The end," she said, " will not be happy. At least, I dare not believe it; but perhaps the end is a long way off. Perhaps I shall die *before* becoming unhappy. Promise me nothing, but listen to the promise that I make to you to love you for ever. Even if you cease to love *me* I shall not cease to love *you*. May the moment that you have to complain of my love be the last moment of my life! Come with me, come and sit on the same bench where we spoke for the first time. Twenty times before then I had approached you, but I had not dared to speak to you. That day I was bolder. Blessings on that day; and my boldness! Blessings on the spot where that bench was placed! I will plant a rose tree there and some jasmin and honeysuckle."

And in fact she planted them. They grew and

flourished, and those are the only traces that remain of a love that was once so sweet.

If only I could depict for you, madam, all her amiability, all her indefinable charm! If only I could portray for you the tenderness, the skill, with which she met love with love; mastering the senses with the soul, putting sweeter pleasures in the place of livelier ones, making me forget her person in her grace, her wit, and her talents. Sometimes I used to complain of her reserve, which I called hardness and indifference; then she replied that my father would perhaps permit me some day to marry her; and, when I wished to implore him immediately for this permission, she would say, " Until we have asked for it, we can have the happiness of believing that it will not be refused."

Thus nourished with love and hope, I lived as happily as a man *can* live when he is without tranquillity, and when his heart is filled with a passion which he has long regarded as unworthy of occupying it.

" Oh, my brother, my brother, what would you say? " I cried to myself at times. " But you I have no longer, and who could be worthier than Caliste to take your place? "

My days did not, however, pass in complete idleness. The regiment in which I served having been involved in the disaster of Saratoga, it would have been necessary, if they had decided to send me back to America, to enroll me in another corps;

but my father, made all the more unhappy at
having lost one son, by not approving the war,
swore that the other should never return to it, and,
profiting by the circumstance of the capitulation of
Saratoga, said that as my ill-health alone had
separated me from my regiment, I must be considered as belonging to an army which could no
longer serve against the Americans. Having thus,
after a fashion, left the service, although I had not
yet discarded the uniform or relinquished my
commission, I began to prepare myself for a
Parliamentary and civil career; and, in order to
play a distinguished part, I resolved that, together
with the studying of the laws and history of my
country, I would learn to express myself with
elegance in my own language. I defined eloquence
as the power of persuading where one cannot
convince, and this power appeared to me necessary
with so many people and on so many occasions
that I did not think it possible to be at too great
pains to acquire it. Following the example of the
famous Lord Chatham, I set myself to translating
Cicero and, above all, Demosthenes, burning my
translations and recommencing them a hundred
times. Caliste aided me to find the best words and
phrases, although she understood neither Greek
nor Latin; but, when I had translated my author
literally to her, I perceived that she often grasped
his thought better than I myself; and when I
translated Pascal or Bossuet, she was of even
greater assistance. For fear of neglecting the

occupations that I had prescribed to myself, we regulated the employment of each day, and when, forgetting myself at her side, I passed one with which I was not satisfied, she made me pay a fine for the benefit of her poor *protégés*. I rose betimes; the morning hours were devoted to walking with Caliste. Hours all too short; ravishing hours where everything appeared beautiful and animated to two united hearts, to two hearts that were both tranquil and enchanted. For Nature is a third person whom lovers *can* love, and who can claim a share in their admiration without chilling their emotion for each other. The remainder of my time until dinner was employed in study. I dined at home, but I drank coffee at her house. I would find her dressed; I would show her what I had done, and when I was at all satisfied with it, after having corrected it with her, I would copy it at her dictation. Afterwards I would read her any novelty that had some reputation or, if nothing new excited our curiosity, I would read her Voltaire, Rousseau, Fénélon, Buffon, all that is best and most pleasing in your language. Then I would go to the public rooms, for fear, she said, that people might think that, in order to keep me more securely, she had buried me. After having passed there an hour or two, I was permitted to return and not to quit her again that day. According to the season we walked or conversed, or made music, until supper, except on those days of the week when we had a real concert.

I heard the ablest English and foreign musicians display at her house all their art and give expression to all their genius; they were more moved to emulation by the attention and sensibility of Caliste than by the recompenses of the great. She invited no one; but sometimes men of the highest rank obtained leave to come. On one occasion some ladies sought the same permission; but it was denied them. Another time some young men, hearing the music, made bold to enter. Caliste said to them that they had doubtless come in error and might remain if they observed complete silence, but that she begged them not to return without having first informed her. You perceive, madam, that she knew how to make herself respected; and her lover himself was only the most submissive as well as the most enchanted of her admirers.

After the concerts we used to give a supper to our musicians and amateurs. I was permitted to bear the cost of these suppers; and it was the only privilege of that nature which I ever enjoyed. Never were there gayer repasts. Englishmen, Germans, Italians, all our " virtuosos " mixed fantastically enough their languages, their pastimes, their prejudices, their habits, and their sallies of wit. With any other women than Caliste these suppers would have been stiff, or would have degenerated into orgies; with her they were decent, gay, and charming.

Caliste having found that, when we were alone,

the hour following supper was the most difficult
to employ prudently, except when moonlight
invited us to walk out, or the wit of an author
tempted us to finish a book, conceived the idea of
summoning on these occasions a little violon-
cellist, dirty and drunken, but very gifted. An
imperceptible sign to her lackey would evoke this
little gnome. At the moment when I saw him
appear, as if out of the ground, I would curse him
and move to go away; but a look or a smile from
Caliste would check me, and, often, with my hat
on my head and leaning against the door, I would
remain motionless, listening to the ravishing
sounds produced by her harpsichord and voice,
together with the instrument of this evil genius.
At other times I would take, not without grumb-
ling, my harp or my violin, and play until Caliste
dismissed us both. Thus passed weeks, months,
more than a year; and you see that even the memory of this enchanted time has rekindled a spark
of gaiety in a heart overwhelmed by grief.

At length I received a letter from my father; he
had been told that my health, perfectly recovered,
no longer demanded my residence at Bath and he
spoke of my returning home and marrying a young
person of whom the fortune, the birth, and the
education were all that could be desired. I replied
that in truth my health *was* restored, and, after
speaking of her to whom I owed it, and whom I
frankly called the mistress of the late Lord L——,
I said that I would marry no one unless he would

permit me to marry her. I implored him not to be swayed by a prejudice that might make him reject my petition, and begged him to inform himself in London, in Bath, everywhere, of the character and conduct of her whom I wished to give him as a daughter. *Yes, " of her conduct,"* I repeated, " and if you hear that, before the death of her lover she was ever found wanting in decorum, or, since his death, has ever suffered the least impertinence, if you ever hear anything but eulogies or blessings, I will renounce my dearest hope, the only thing which causes me to regard life and the preservation and recovery of my reason, as a benefit."

This is the answer that I received from my father.

" You are of age, my son, and can marry without my consent; as to my approval, you can never have that for the marriage of which you speak, and, if you contract it, I shall never see you again. I have not sought for preferment, and you know that I have let the younger branch of our family solicit and obtain a title without making the least effort to procure one for ourselves; but honour is as dear to me as to any man, and never, with my consent, shall my honour or that of my family be impeached. I shudder at the thought of a daughter-in-law before whom one would not dare to speak of chastity, to whose children I could not counsel chastity without causing their mother to blush. And would you also not blush, when I exhorted them to prefer honour to their passions,

and not to permit these to overcome or to sub-
jugate them? No, my son; I will *not* give the
place of the wife I adored to such a daughter-in-
law. Your mother's name it is in your power to
give her, and perhaps you will make me die of
sorrow in doing so, for I shudder at the mere idea;
but, so long as I live, she shall not sit in your
mother's place. You know that the birth of my
children cost me their mother; you know that the
devotion of my sons to each other cost me one of
them; it lies with you to decide if you desire that
my remaining son should be separated from us by
an insane passion; for I will have no son if he can
take such a wife."

Caliste, when she saw me return to her later than
was my usual habit, and with an air of distress,
at once divined the import of the letter; and,
having compelled me to give it her, she read it,
and I saw every word pierce her heart like a
dagger.

"Do not let us altogether despair," she said,
"allow me to write to him to-morrow; at present
I could not."

Then, seating herself upon the sofa beside me,
she bent over me weeping and caressing me with
an abandonment that she had never shown before.
She well knew that I was myself too much overcome to take advantage of it.

I have translated to the best of my ability
Caliste's letter, and I will here transcribe it.

"Suffer, sir, an unhappy woman to appeal from

your judgment to your heart, and to venture to
plead her cause before you. I feel but too well the
force of your reasoning, but deign to consider, sir,
if there are not some considerations also in *my*
favour which may be opposed to those that
condemn me. Think first whether the most complete devotion, the liveliest tenderness, the most
sincere gratitude, should not bear some weight in
the balance that I myself desire you to hold and to
consult on this occasion. Deign to ask yourself if
your son could expect these sentiments from any
other woman in the degree to which I hold and
shall always hold them, and let your fancy depict
for you, if it can, all that they would enable me to
do and to endure. Then consider other marriages,
such marriages as now appear to you the most
suitable and advantageous, and, if you discover in
almost all of them inconveniences and vexations
yet greater and more apparent than those that you
fear in the marriage which your son desires, will
you not then support with more indulgence the
thought of the one, and desire less ardently the
others? Ah! if honourable birth, a pure life, and
an unsullied name were all that was needed to
make your son happy; if virtue were all; if faithful love were nothing, do you not think that my
generosity, or rather my love, would not suffice to
silence for ever the only desire, the only ambition
of my heart?

" You think me, above all, unworthy of being
the mother of your grandchildren. I submit

myself with tears to your judgment, based as it is
on that of the world. If you were to consult but
your own promptings, if you were to condescend
to see and to know me, your verdict might
perhaps be less severe. You would see with what
docility I should repeat to them your lessons,
lessons which I have indeed not followed, but
which were never given to *me*; and, even supposing that on my lips they should lose part of
their force, you would at least see that my conduct
offered a constant example of virtue. Debased as I
may seem to you, believe me, sir, that no woman,
of whatever rank or whatever condition, ever was
more sheltered than I have been from any licen-
tious sights or speech. Ah, sir! is it impossible to
you to form even a slightly favourable idea of one
who has attached herself to your son with so
tender a love? I conclude by vowing to you never
to consent to anything which you condemn, even
if your son should entertain the thought; but it is
not possible that he should do so; he will not for
one moment forget the respect he owes you.
Permit me, sir, to share that sentiment at least, and
do not refuse from me its humble and sincere
expression! ''

While awaiting my father's reply, all our conversation was of Caliste's parents, her education,
her journeys, indeed, of her whole history. I put
her questions which I had never before asked. I
had sought to spare her recollections which might
be painful to her; she now put an end to my

scruples and precautions. I longed to fathom everything; and, as if that could be of any assist-ance to our hopes, I took infinite delight in dis-covering how much she gained by being more perfectly known. Alas! it was not *I* that was to be persuaded! She told me that, by reason of her lover's extreme consideration, no one, man or woman, in any country, could *affirm* that she had been his mistress. She told me that she had never suffered from him a single rebuff, a single moment of ill-temper or discontent or even neglect. What qualities must have been hers that a man, her lover, her benefactor, nay, her master, could treat her for eight years as a divinity! I asked her one day if she had ever entertained the thought of leaving him.

" Yes," she said, " I did consider it once, but I was so much struck by the ingratitude of such a design that I would not permit myself to perceive its wisdom; I thought myself the dupe of a phantom that called itself virtue but was indeed vice, and I rejected it with horror."

During the three days that my father's answer tarried, I had her permission to desert my books and society. I was with her from early morning; sorrow had made us more familiar without making us less prudent. On the fourth day Caliste received this reply. Without copying it or translating it, madam, I send it you; you can translate it if you wish your own daughter to read it some day; I have not the strength to do so.

" MADAM,

"I regret finding myself under the compulsion of saying disobliging things to a person of your sex, and, I will add, of your merit; for, without having informed myself about you, which would have been useless, as I could not be swayed by what I learnt, I have nevertheless heard much of you that is creditable. Once more I regret having to say disobliging things to you; but to leave your letter without a reply would be even more uncivil than to confute it. It is therefore the latter course that I find myself compelled to take.

"First, madam, I might say that I have no other proofs of your attachment to my son than what you yourself tell me, together with a connection that does not always demonstrate a very great attachment; but, supposing this attachment to be indeed as great as you affirm (and I admit that I incline to believe it), why should I not think that another woman might love my son as much as you do, and, even supposing that another woman, whom he might marry, should *not* love him with an equal tenderness and devotion, is it certain that such a degree of partiality is a great benefit to him, and is it clear to you that he has need of such great sacrifices from a woman? But I will suppose that it *is* a great good; even then, is such an attachment everything? You speak to me of the disorder that one sees in most establishments; but is it sound reasoning to resign oneself to suffering *certain* disadvantages because elsewhere there are *probable* ones? to ignore the disadvantages that one sees clearly, in order to avoid those that one cannot as yet foresee, and to take a definitely bad decision because there might be worse? You ask if it is impossible for me to entertain a good opinion of her who loves my son; you might add ' and who is beloved by him '? No; without doubt, and I entertain so good an opinion of you that I believe that you would, in truth, set a good example to your children, and that, far from refuting the lessons that might be given them, you would give them the same lessons, and perhaps with more zeal and care than another. But do you not understand that in a hundred circumstances I should conceive you to be suffering from what was said or not said to your children and on a hundred other subjects? And do you not realize that the more you might attach me by your goodness, your virtues, and your amiable qualities, the more I should suffer in seeing, in imagining that *you* were suffering, and that you had not the happiness or the respect which, in many regards, you deserved? Indeed, madam, I should blame myself did I fail in the most affectionate consideration towards you; and yet it would be impossible for me to entertain such a feeling except perhaps for the few moments, when I might forget that this handsome, amiable, and virtuous woman was my daughter-in-law. But, so soon as I heard you named what I had heard my wife and mother named (pardon my frankness, madam), my heart

would turn against you, and I should perhaps hate
you for having been so amiable that my son was
able to love and to marry you. And if, at such a
moment, I thought to hear anyone speaking of my
son or his children, I should conceive them to be
saying, ' He is the husband, they are the children
of a woman of that sort.' Indeed, madam, that
would be intolerable; for, even now, when there
is no reality in the idea, I find it insupportable.

" Do not believe, nevertheless, that I feel any
contempt for your person. It would be very
unjust to feel it, and I am disposed to a quite
contrary sentiment. The promise which you make
at the end of your letter places me under an obligation to you, and I do not blush to be obliged.
I have, I know not why, a complete trust in that
promise. To recompense you for your goodness,
and for the respect that you show to the sentiment
that unites a son and his father, I promise to you
as well as to my son, to make no attempt to
separate you, and not to be the first to speak to him
of any marriage, even were a princess proposed to
me as a daughter-in-law, on the condition that
neither he nor you ever speak to me again of the
marriage now in question. If I allowed myself
to be persuaded I know that I should have the
most bitter regrets; and, if I resisted further
entreaties, as I certainly should, in addition to the
sorrow of wounding a son whom I love tenderly,
and who deserves my love, I should perhaps be
preparing for myself future remorse. For an

affectionate father often reproaches himself without reason for not having yielded to even the most irrational entreaties of his child. Believe, madam, that it is not without pain, even now, that I am the cause of suffering both to him and to you."

I found Caliste seated on the ground, her head pressed against the marble of the mantelpiece.

" This is the twentieth seat that I have tried this last hour," she said. " I am remaining here because my head is burning."

She pointed with her finger to my father's letter, which lay open on the sofa. I sat down, and while I read she, having shifted her place a little, leaned her head on my knees. Absorbed in my own thoughts, regretting the past, fearing the future, and not knowing how to arrange the present, I scarcely saw or felt her. At length I raised her and made her be seated. Our tears flowed together.

" Let us at least be to each other all that we *can* be," I said to her, speaking very low, and almost as if I feared that she might hear me. I was able to remain in doubt whether she had heard me or not; to believe for a moment that she might consent, for she did not answer and her eyes remained closed.

" Let us change, Caliste," I said, " this sad moment to a moment of rapture."

" Ah," she replied, opening her eyes and casting upon me looks of sorrow and fear, " I must then become again what I once was."

" No," I said, after some moments of silence.

" You *need* do nothing; but I *believed* you to love me."

" And do I then *not* love you? " she said, putting in her turn her arms around me, " do I then *not* love you? "

Imagine, madam, if you can, what was passing in my heart. At length I threw myself at her feet, I embraced her knees, I implored forgiveness for my impetuosity.

" I *know* that you love me," I said. " I respect and adore you; you shall be to me only what you desire to be."

" Ah," she said, " I see very well that I must either once more become that which is horrible to me to be, or else I must lose you, and that would be a thousand times more horrible."

" No," I answered, " you are mistaken, you affront me; you will *not* lose me, I shall always love you."

" You will always love me," she went on, " but I shall nevertheless lose you. And what right have I indeed to keep you? I shall lose you, I know."

Her tears seemed about to choke her; but, for fear that I should summon assistance, for fear of not remaining alone with me, she promised to make every effort to calm herself; and at length she was successful.

From that moment Caliste was no longer the same; uneasy when she did not see me, trembling when I left her, as if she feared never to see me again; overcome with joy at my return; fearing always to displease me, and weeping with delight when in any way she had given me pleasure, she was sometimes more lovable, more touching, more ravishing, than ever before; but she had lost that serenity, that evenness of temper, that nice propriety which had previously always been hers, and had distinguished her so much. She attempted indeed to do the same things, and they were indeed the same things that she did; but, done sometimes absently and sometimes with passion, sometimes with lassitude, always better or less well than before, they produced the same effect neither on herself nor on others.

Ah! heaven! What torments and struggles did she not undergo! Moved by my least caresses, which she now sought rather than averted, and always on her guard against her own emotions; seeking to attract me as if by policy and from the fear that I should escape her altogether, and then reproaching herself for having attracted me; fear and tenderness, passion and reserve succeeded each other in her looks and movements with such rapidity that they appeared to govern her simultaneously. Scorn, admiration, and pity affected me in turns; kindled and frozen, teased, enchanted, and touched, I was plunged into inconceivable agitation.

" Let us make an end," I said one day, carried away both by love and anger. I locked her door and led her from the harpsichord.

"You will not, I know, do me any violence," she said gently, "for you are my master."

Her speech and her tone quieted my vehemence, and I could only seat her on my knees, support her head on my shoulder, and, moistening her beautiful hands with my tears, ask her forgiveness again and again. She continued to pour out her thanks to me in a manner that showed the reality of her alarm. Yet her passion and her suffering were in truth equal to my own, and she would have *liked* to be my mistress.

One day I said to her, "You cannot decide to give yourself, and yet you wish that you had given yourself."

"That is quite true," she said.

But there was nothing more for me to obtain, or even to attempt, from this avowal.

Do not apprehend, madam, that all our moments were painful, and that our situation did not still have its charms; for, indeed, it had many which arose perhaps from its strangeness, and from our privations. The smallest tokens of love kept their full worth. We never did each other the least service without joy. To beg a favour was our manner of expiating an offence, or of causing a quarrel to be forgotten; it was the way we always chose, and never in vain. Her caresses, in truth, procured me more apprehension than pleasure, but the intimacy that there was between us was delicious to us both. I was treated sometimes as a brother, or rather as a sister, and this privilege I never ceased to hold dear.

Caliste became subject, you will not be surprised
to learn, to terrible sleeplessness. I disapproved
of her taking remedies which might have completed the ruin of her health; so I decided that her
maid and I, by reading aloud to her by turns,
should assist her to sleep. When we saw her
sleeping, we—I as scrupulously as Fanny—withdrew, as noiselessly as possible; and the following
day I would obtain for myself in recompense the
permission to recline at her feet, with her knees
as my pillow, and to sleep thus when I could.

One night I fell asleep while reading at her
bedside; and Fanny, when she brought her
mistress's breakfast as usual at daybreak—the
nights were made as short as possible—approached
quietly and did not waken me immediately. The
light grew brighter; I opened my eyes at length
and saw the woman smiling at me.

" You see," I said to Fanny, " all is just as you
left it, the table, the lamp, the book fallen from
my hands on to my knees."

" Yes, indeed," she replied, and, on seeing me
embarrassed as to how to leave the house, " Walk
boldly away, sir; and even if the neighbours see
you, do not distress yourself. They know that my
mistress is ill, and we have told them so often that
you live together as brother and sister that if we
now told them the contrary, they would not credit
us."

" And do they not laugh at me? " I asked.

" Oh, no, sir; they were merely astonished;
you are both of you respected and beloved."

" So they are astonished, Fanny," I went on, " in truth they well may be. And if we astonished them less would they then cease to love us? "

" Ah, sir, it would be quite different."

" I cannot believe it, Fanny," I cried, " but in any case, if they did not know it. . . ."

" Such things, sir," she said ingenuously, " in order to be concealed . . . must not be."

" But——"

" There is no ' but,' sir; you could not hide it so well from James and me that *we* should not guess at it. James would *say* nothing, but he would no longer serve madam as he now serves her, that is like the first lady in the land, which proves that he respects his mistress; and I, I also, should *say* nothing, but I could not remain with madam, for I should think, ' if it becomes known some day, it will be held up to me all the rest of my life.' Then other servants, who have always heard me praise madam, would suspect something, and the neighbours, who know how good and amiable she is, would also suspect, and then another waiting-woman, who would not love madam as I do, would come, and very soon there would be talk. There are so many tongues that *want* to talk. Whether they praise or blame is all one to them, so long as they talk. I seem to hear them already. ' You see,' they will say, ' never trust appearances again! It was such a fine reformation! She gave to the poor, she went to church.' What is admired at present could then perhaps be regarded as hypocrisy. And, sir, they would forgive you even less than madam; for, seeing how much she loves you, they would think you ought to have married her, and they would always say: ' Why did he not marry her? ' "

" Ah Fanny, Fanny," exclaimed Caliste sadly, " you speak but too truly. What have I been about? " she added in French. " Why did I leave it to Fanny to prove to you that it is no longer in my power to change my conduct even if it were my desire."

I wished to reply, but she begged me to leave her.

A neighbouring shopkeeper, earlier astir than the others, was already opening his shop. I passed close to him in order not to appear desirous of escaping notice. " How is madam? " he asked.

" She scarcely sleeps at all," I answered. " We read to her every evening, Fanny and I, for an hour or more before we are able to put her to sleep, and she wakes with the dawn. Last night I read so long that I fell asleep myself."

" Have you breakfasted, sir? " he asked me.

" No," I answered. " I intend to throw myself on my bed now, and to sleep for an hour or so."

" That would be almost a pity, sir," he said. " The weather is so fine and you do not look tired or drowsy. Come, rather, and take breakfast with me in my garden."

I accepted the invitation, flattering myself that this man would surely be the last of the neighbours to slander Caliste; and he spoke to me of her, and of all the good that she did and never told me of, with so much pleasure and admiration that I was amply repaid for my complaisance.

That very day Caliste received a letter from the uncle of her former lover, who was constantly praying her to visit him in London. I resolved to pass the time of her absence at my father's; and we left Bath at the same hour.

"Shall I ever see you again?" she asked. "Is it certain that I shall ever see you again?"

"Yes," I said; "and as soon as you wish it, unless I am dead."

We promised each other to write at least twice a week, and never was promise better kept. Since we neither of us ever had an experience or a thought that we should not willingly have shared with the other our difficulty lay rather in *not* writing.

My father might perhaps have greeted me coldly if he had not been very well satisfied with the manner in which I had employed my time. He had received information from others besides myself, and fortunately he had with him people capable, in his opinion, of judging me, and whose approval I gained. They thought that I had acquired some little knowledge and facility in expressing myself, and they prophesied for me a success which flattered a father, already disposed to regard me with a tender partiality. I made acquaintance with the paternal mansion, which had only visited for a

few moments since my return from America, and
that at a time when I paid heed to nothing. I
made acquaintance also with my father's friends
and neighbours. I shot and hunted with them, and
I was happy enough to please them.

" I saw you on your return from America," one
of the oldest of our family friends said to me; " if
your father truly owes to a woman the pleasure of
seeing you as you are at present he ought to let
you marry her out of gratitude." The ladies whom
I chanced to meet gave me a flattering reception.
How much easier it was to succeed with some of
those whom my father most respected than with
the girl that he despised! And I admit that my
heart had so great a need of repose that, at some
moments, any means of obtaining it would have
seemed good to me, for Caliste had shown herself
so little inclined to jealousy that the idea that I
might pain her never occurred to me. I did not
realize that every distraction was an infidelity;
and, seeing no one to be compared with her, it
never entered my mind that I might become really
unfaithful to her. Yet so I can truthfully affirm
that I preferred any distraction to that afforded by
the society of women.

I grew impatient at times to make a larger and
more practical use of my faculties than I had done
hitherto. I did not as yet suspect the pursuit of
the public good to be only a chimera, or realize
that fortune, circumstances, and events, which no
one can anticipate or affect, alter nations without

either ameliorating or injuring them, while the intentions of the most virtuous citizen have scarcely ever influenced the well-being of his country. I did not as yet perceive the slave of ambition to be still more puerile and more unhappy than the slave of a woman. My father insisted that I should offer myself for a seat in Parliament at the first election and, enchanted to be able for once to please him, I consented with joy. Caliste wrote to me.

" If I be of any consequence in your plans, as I still dare to flatter myself that I am, you cannot fail to embrace a project that will compel you to live in London. An uncle of my father, who desired to see me, has just informed me that I have given him more happiness in eight days than all his own relatives and their children in twenty years, and that he intends to leave me his house and his fortune. I shall know, he believes, how to repair and to embellish the one and to make good use of the other, while his other relatives would only destroy and dissipate dully, or save shabbily. I tell you all this so that you should not blame me for not having opposed his wish; I have, besides, as much right as anyone to this inheritance, and those whom he might otherwise remember are not in need. My relative is rich and very old: his house is very well situated near Whitehall. I admit that the notion of receiving you there or of lending it to you affords me prodigious satisfaction. If you conceive any costly fancy or covet a very fine horse or picture I beg you to gratify yourself, for his will is made and the testator so obstinate that he will assuredly not reconsider it; so that I think myself rich from this moment and should very much like to become your creditor."

In another letter she wrote: "While I find it exceedingly tedious away from you, and all that I do appears to me useless or insipid unless I can connect it with you in some way or other, I perceive that you are finding repose away from me. On the one side tedium and impatience, on the other satisfaction and refreshment; what a contrast! I do not, however, complain. If I were distressed I should not dare to say so. Were I to see another woman come between us I should distress myself far more and yet it would not be right to say it, and I should not venture to do so."

In yet another letter she wrote: "I believe myself to have seen your father. Struck by his countenance, which resembled yours, I remained motionless, regarding him. It was surely he; and he, also, looked at me."

In truth, my father, as he has since told me, *had* seen her by chance during a visit which he had made to London. I do not know where he had met her, but he enquired who that beautiful woman could be.

"What!" someone said to him, "you do not know the Caliste of Lord L—— and of your own son!"

"Without that first name . . ." he said to me,

and then hesitated. "Wretch! oh why did you utter it?"

I began to grow uneasy concerning my means of returning to Bath. My health was no longer either a reason or a pretext, and, although I had nothing to retain me elsewhere, it would appear strange for me to commence another sojourn there. Caliste felt this, herself, and in a letter in which she announced to me her departure from London, showed me her disquiet. In the same letter she told me of some new acquaintance whom she had made at the house of the uncle of Lord L——, all of whom were talking of going to Bath. "It would be terrible," she added, "to see everyone there except the only person in the world whom I desire to see."

Fortunately (at least, at that moment I thought it to be fortunate) my father, curious perhaps in his heart to know her whom he was rejecting, and to hear her spoken of with precision and in detail, wishing, too, it may be, to continue to live with me without causing me any sacrifice, and, possibly, even to make my stay in Bath seem the more natural (for many motives may be united in one intention), my father, I say, announced that he was going to pass some months at Bath. I had difficulty in concealing from him my excessive joy. "Heaven!" I said to myself, "if only I could unite everything, my father, my duty, Caliste, her happiness and mine!"

Scarcely, however, had my father's project

become known when a lady, the widow since some months of one of our relatives, wrote to him saying that, as she wished to go to Bath with her son, a boy of nine or ten years of age, she begged him to take a house where they could all reside together. My father's notions appeared to me to be disturbed by this proposition, but I could not divine whether it was agreeable or disagreeable to him. Whichever was the case he could not but acquiesce, and I was despatched to Bath to arrange a lodging for my father, for this unknown cousin, her son, and myself.

Caliste had already returned. Enchanted with doing anything in my company, she directed and shared my activities with a zeal worthy of a better cause, and when my father and Lady Betty B——— arrived, they admired in all that they saw round them an elegance, a taste, which they declared to surpass anything that they had ever seen, and they showed me a gratitude which I assuredly did not deserve. Caliste, on this occasion, had worked against her own interests; for certainly Lady Betty, from that moment, attributed to me intentions which her fortune, her face, and her age made exceedingly natural. She had married very young and was only seventeen at the time of the birth of her son, Sir Harry. I do not therefore blame her for the ideas that she conceived, nor for the conduct which was their consequence. What *does* astonish me is the impression that her good opinion made upon me. I was not excessively flattered, but I *was* rendered less sensible to Caliste's attachment. She became less precious to me. I believed that all women loved, and that chance more than anything else determined the object of a passion to which they were all previously inclined. Caliste did not delay in seeing that I was changed. . . . " Changed! " No, I was not. That word says too much; for nothing of that which I have just expressed was clearly in my thought or my heart. Oh why, mobile and inconsequent creatures that we are, do we attempt to account for ourselves? I did not then perceive that I *was* changed, and now, to account for my heedlessness, my security, my indolent and feeble behaviour, I attribute its cause to an alteration that I did not at that time realize.

Lady Betty's son, a little boy of about ten, was a charming child and resembled my brother. He sometimes reminded me of him and of our childish games so vividly that my eyes would fill with tears as I looked at him. He became my pupil and my companion; I never walked out without him and I took him almost every day to visit Caliste.

One day when I had gone alone to her I found there a country gentleman of a handsome appearance who was watching her draw. I concealed my surprise and annoyance. I desired to sit him out, but that proved impossible, for he asked her to give him supper. At eleven o'clock I said that nothing agreed with her so ill as retiring late, and compelled my rival (yes, he *was* my rival) to withdraw, together with myself. For the first time the hours with Caliste had seemed to me long. The man's name was not unknown to me; it was a name that none of those who had borne it had rendered illustrious; but his family was ancient and had long been of some consequence in a northern county of England. He knew Lord L——'s uncle, and having seen Caliste with him at the opera, he had desired to be presented to her and had even asked leave to visit her. He had been to see her two or three times and believed he had found in real life one of those Muses or Graces that he had only before heard of in books. After his third visit he went to the general to gather information about Caliste, her fortune, and her family. He was answered with all possible frankness.

" You are a man of honour, sir," said Caliste's admirer; " would you advise me to marry her? "

" Undoubtedly," was the reply, " if you can. I should give the same advice to my son, or to the son of my dearest friend. There is a dolt who has loved her for a long time and who does not dare to marry her because his father, who will not even see her from fear of being prepossessed in her favour, will not give his consent. They will repent during the rest of their lives; but you had better make haste, for they might change their minds."

That was the man whom I had found with Caliste. The following day I was with her very early and expressed my annoyance and impatience of the day before.

" What! " she said, " *That* pained you? In old days I used to see well enough that you could not bear to find anyone with me, even a workman or a woman; but for some time you have not failed to bring the little baronet with you, and I thought that it was in order that we should not be alone together."

" But," I said, " he is a child."

" He hears and sees as well as another," she replied.

" And if I do not bring him any more," I said, " will you then cease to receive the man who vexed me yesterday? "

" You may bring the child whenever you want to," she said, " but I cannot dismiss the gentleman you refer to so long as no one has a higher claim on me than the benefactor who made me acquainted with him, and who prayed me to receive him kindly."

" He is in love with you," I said, pacing up and down the room with great strides, " *he* has no father, *he* might . . ."

I could not finish. Caliste made no reply; the gentleman in question was announced, and I went away. Soon afterwards I returned in order to accustom myself to him rather than be banished from my home—for it *was* my home. After that I went there even oftener than was my habit, but remained less time. Sometimes she was alone, and that was a happiness in which my whole being rejoiced. I no longer took the little boy who, after a few days, bitterly complained of this. One day, in Lady Betty's presence, he addressed his complaints to my father, and begged him to take him to Mistress Caliste as I no longer did so. The name and his way of saying it made my father smile with mingled kindliness and embarrassment.

" I do not go there myself," he said to Sir Harry.

" Is it that your son will not take *you* there either? " the child continued. " Ah, if you had been there once or twice, you could go back there every day like him."

Seeing my father softened and affected I was on the point of throwing myself at his feet; but the presence of Lady Betty, or my unlucky star, or rather my miserable weakness, restrained me. Oh, Caliste! How much more courageous would you not have been! You would have made use of this happy chance; you would have attempted something and would have succeeded, and we might have passed together the life that we have not been able to learn to pass apart!

While, uncertain, irresolute, I was permitting this unique moment to escape me, a servant came from Caliste, to whom I had repeated Sir Harry's complaints, to ask my lady if the child might dine with her. The little boy did not even wait for the answer; he ran to throw himself on James's neck, beseeching to be taken immediately. That evening, the next day, the following day he talked so much about my mistress that he made Lady Betty impatient and began to interest my father in good earnest. Who knows what that kind of intercession might not have effected? But my father was compelled to go and spend several days at home on urgent affairs, and the current of good will, once checked, could not be set in motion again.

Sir Harry made himself so much at home at Caliste's that I no longer found her alone with her new suitor. He was, I think, as much incommoded by the child, as I was by *him*. Caliste, in this situation, displayed an art, and resources of talent, wit, and kindness such as I had never imagined possible. The Norfolk squire, not being able to converse freely with her, desired at least that she should charm him, as in London, with her voice and her harpsichord, and asked for French and Italian airs and operatic pieces; but Caliste, thinking all that to be familiar to me and tedious for the little boy, and that I should also care very little to help her to her effects by accompanying her, as used to be my habit, set herself to inventing songs of which she herself composed the music and I the words, and which she had sung by the child and judged by my rival. She sang and played and made variations on the charming ballad " Have you see my Hannah? " in such a way as to draw tears from me a score of times. She also wished to teach Sir Harry to draw, and, in order to escape without awkwardness from this incessant music, she obtained some pictures of Rubens and Snyders, where children are playing with garlands of flowers, and, copying these with the aid of a poor but talented artist, she surrounded her room with them, leaving only space for consoles on which were to be placed classical lamps and porcelain vases. This work occupied us all, and if the child alone was satisfied by it, everyone was entertained. Astonished myself at the excellence of the effect when the apartment was arranged, and thinking that she had never before shown so much activity or invention, I had the cruelty to ask her whether it was in order to render her home more agreeable to Mr. M——.

" Ungrateful wretch! " she said.

" Yes," I cried; " you are right, I *am* an ungrateful wretch; but who indeed could endure, without ill-humour, to see talents, which he used to enjoy alone, daily displayed to others with even greater brilliance? "

" It is, in truth," she said, " their swan song."

A knock was heard at the door.

" Prepare to see," said little Harry, as if he had understood more than had been said, " our indefatigable Norfolk gentleman."

His guess proved right.

For some days longer we went on with this life, but it was not in my rival's plans to share Caliste permanently with a child and me. He came to tell her one morning that, after what he had learned of her from General D—— and from public opinion, but, above all, from what he had himself seen, he was resolved to follow the inclination of his heart and to offer her his hand and his fortune.

"I am going," he said, "to take an exact cognisance of all my affairs, in order to render you an account of them. I wish the General, your friend and protector, to whom I owe the happiness of knowing you, to examine it and to decide with you whether my offer is worthy of acceptance; but, when you have examined everything, I know you to be too generous to make me wait long for a definite reply, and, should I find you and the General together, only a few moments would be required to decide my fate."

"I wish that I were myself more worthy of your proposals," replied Caliste, who was as much agitated as if she had not indeed expected this declaration. "Go now, sir; I am sensible of all the honour that you do me. I will examine myself to see whether I can accept your offer, and, on your return, I shall quickly be resolved."

Sir Harry and I found her an hour later so pale, so changed, that we grew alarmed. Is it credible that I did not, even then, come to a decision? I needed assuredly only to have said one word. I passed three days, almost from morning to night, with Caliste, looking at her, dreaming, hesitating, and yet I said nothing. The day before that on which her suitor was to return I went to her in the afternoon. I went alone. I knew that her maid had gone to visit some relatives a few miles distant from Bath and was only to return the

following day. I found Caliste holding a casket
filled with small trinkets, engraved gems, and
miniatures which she had brought back from
Italy or which my lord had given her. She compelled me to look at them, and she remarked those
which most pleased me. She placed on my finger
a ring which my lord had always worn and begged
me to keep it. She said scarcely anything. She
was excessively tender but resigned and sad.

" You did not make any promise to that man? "
I asked.

" None," she said, and that is the only word that
I can recall of an evening that I have recollected a
thousand times. But never in all my life shall I
forget the manner in which we parted. I looked
at my watch. " What! " I said, " it is already nine
o'clock." And I moved to go away.

" Please stay! " she said.

" It is not in my power," I replied, " my father
and Lady Betty are expecting me."

" You will take supper so many times yet with
them," she said.

" Then," I said, " you will then never take
supper again? "

" Yes, I shall take supper."

" They have promised me ices."

" I will give them you." (The weather was
prodigiously hot.)

She was very lightly clad. She placed herself in
front of the door towards which I was advancing;
I embraced her, and removed her a little from it.

" Then you will *not* stay? " she said.

" You are cruel," I said, " to appeal to me in this way."

" I!—cruel! "

I opened the door, I went out; she watched me go, and I heard her say on shutting it: " *It is all over.*"

Those words haunted me. After having heard them hundreds of times I went back in half an hour to ask for their explanation. I found her door locked. She called to me from a dressing-room that lay beyond her room, that she had entered the bath and could not open to me, having nobody with her.

" But," I said, " supposing something should happen to you."

" Nothing *will* happen to me," she said.

" Can I be quite sure," I asked, " that you harbour no sinister design? "

" Quite sure," she said. " Is there any other world where I should find you? But I am making myself hoarse and must not shout any more."

I returned home a little easier; but that " *It is all over* " would not leave my mind, and will never leave it, although I did see Caliste again. The next morning I went back to her. Fanny told me that she could not receive me; and, following me to the road: " What has come to my mistress? " she asked. " What sorrow have you caused her? "

" None that I know of," I replied.

" I found her," she said, " in an incredible state.

She did not go to bed laſt night. . . . But I do not dare to delay longer. If it is your fault you will have no peace for the reſt of your life."

She went in and I withdrew, very uneasy. An hour later I returned: Caliſte was gone. They gave me the casket of the previous day and a letter. Here it is:

" When I wished to retain you yeſterday I could not succeed. To-day I send you away, and you obey at the firſt word. I am leaving in order to prevent you from committing further cruelties which would poison the reſt of your life, if you ever came to realize them. I am also sparing myself the tortures of contemplating in detail a misfortune and loss which I feel all the more acutely because I have the right to reproach no one. Keep, in memory of my love, those trifles which you admired yeſterday; you can do this with the less scruple because I have resolved to reserve to myself the moſt complete right over everything that I have had from my lord or his uncle."

How can I describe to you, madam, the imbecile torpor in which I became plunged, and all the puerile, absurd, and confused considerations to which my mind confined itself, as if I had become incapable of any sane view, of any reasonable thought? Was my lethargy a return of the disorder of the brain which the death of my brother had occasioned? I should wish you to believe it, otherwise how could you have the patience to continue reading this? I should wish, above all,

to believe it myself; or else for my memories
of that day to be for ever obliterated. Caliste
had only left half an hour earlier; why did
I not follow her? What retained me? If there are
intelligences who are witnesses of our thoughts,
let *them* tell me what retained me? I seated myself
in the place where Caliste used to write, I seized her
pen, I kissed it, I wept; I thought that I intended
to write; but, teased by the bustle that was pro-
ceeding around me in the ordering of my mistress's
furniture and wardrobe, I soon left the house. I
wandered about the country, and then I went back
to shut myself up at home. At one o'clock that
night I lay down fully dressed; I slept; my
brother, Caliste, a thousand melancholy phantoms,
haunted me; I woke up with a start, all in a sweat;
then, a little recovered, I thought that I would go
and tell Caliste what I had suffered that night, and
the terror my dreams had caused me. *Tell Caliste?*
But she was gone; it was her departure that had
thrown me into that terrible condition; Caliste was
no longer within my reach, she was no longer
mine, she was another's. No; she was not yet
another's; I began to move, to run to and fro, to
call. I ordered my horses; and, while they were
being put into my carriage, I went to awaken her
servants and to ask them if they had heard nothing
of Mr. M——. They told me that he had arrived
at eight the previous evening, and that at ten he
had taken the London road. At that moment my
head grew bewildered, I desired to kill myself,

I confused people and things, I persuaded myself that Caliste was dead. A copious bleeding scarcely gave me back my senses; and I found myself in the arms of my father, who henceforth combined with the tenderest care for my health the desire to conceal, as far as possible, the state to which I had been reduced. Fatal precaution! If that state had been made public, it would perhaps have caused alarm and no one would have desired to unite their lot with mine.

The next day they brought me the casket of the previous day and a letter. My father, who never left me, begged me to let him read it.

" Allow me to see for once," he said, " even if it be too late, what Mistress Caliste really is."

" Read it," I said, " you will certainly see nothing that will not be to her credit."

He read:

" It is now quite certain that you have not followed me. Only three hours ago I still had hope. Now I am happy in thinking that it is no longer possible for you to come, for it could have only the most fatal consequences; but I might still receive a letter. There are yet moments when I deceive myself. Habit is so strong; and it is not possible that you should hate me or that I should be indifferent to you. I still have an hour of freedom. Although all is in readiness I could still retract; but, if I hear nothing from you, I shall not retract. You have no more need of me; your situation beside me was too tedious; you have long been fatigued with it. I have made a laſt attempt. I almoſt believed that you would hold me back or that you would follow me, I will not take credit for the other motives that may have entered into my decision; they are too confused. It is, however, now my intention to seek my own repose and the happiness of another in my new situation, and to conduct myself in such a manner that you will never have to blush for me. Adieu; this laſt hour is passing, and, in an inſtant, they will come to tell me that it is paſt; Adieu, you, for whom I can find no name; for the laſt time; Adieu."

The letter was ſtained with tears; my father's fell on those of Caliſte; mine . . . I know the letter by heart but I can now no longer read it.

Two days later Lady Betty, holding the Gazette, read in the liſt of marriages: Charles M—— of Norfolk, with Maria-Sophia. . . . Yes, she read those words; I had to hear them. Heaven! with Maria Sophia! Caliſte!

I cannot fairly accuse Lady Betty of insensibility on this occasion.

I have reason to believe that she considered Caliſte as a good woman, for her condition, with whom I had lived, and who ſtill loved me although I no longer loved her, and who, seeing that I had detached myself from her and would never marry her had sorrowfully decided to marry herself, so as to make an honourable end. Undoubtedly Lady Betty attributed my sadness to compassion alone,

for, without being at all offended, she formed
merely a higher opinion of my heart. All this was
very natural, and only varied from the truth by
shades, which she had not the means of divining.

Eight days went by, during which it seemed to
me that I had ceased to live. Restless, disordered,
moving about continually as if I were seeking
something and finding nothing, indeed, not
seeking anything, but only desiring to escape from
myself, and to escape in turn from everything that
met my gaze. Ah, madam! what a condition was
mine! And I was to endure one yet more cruel!

One morning, during breakfast, Sir Harry said,
coming up to me, " I see that you are so unhappy
that I am always afraid that you, too, will go away.
Now I have an idea. People advise mamma sometimes to marry again, I would rather have you
than anyone else for my father; then you would
stay with me; or you would take me with you if
you should ever go away."

Lady Betty smiled. She appeared to think that
her son was merely putting me in the way of
making a proposal that I had been considering for
some time. I made no reply. She thought that
this was from embarrassment, from timidity. But
my silence lasted too long. My father answered
for me. " That is a very good idea of yours, my
dear Harry," he said, " and I flatter myself that
some day or other everyone will think the same."

" Some day or other! " said Lady Betty. " You
think me more prudish than I am. I shall not

require so much time in order to adopt an idea which would be agreeable to you, as well as to your son and mine."

My father took my hand and made me leave the room with him.

" Do not punish me," he said, " for not having permitted considerations which appeared to me powerful to give way to those that I thought weak. I may have been blind, but I do not think that I have been hard. Nothing in the world is so dear to me as you. Continue to the end to deserve my tenderness; I may wish that I had not been forced to demand this sacrifice; but, since it *has* been made, turn it into something meritorious for yourself and beneficial to your father; show yourself to be an affectionate and generous son by accepting a marriage which will appear advantageous to everyone but you, and give me grandchildren to interest and occupy my old age and to make up to me for your mother, your brother, and yourself; for you never have belonged and perhaps never will belong to yourself, to me, or to reason."

I went back to the breakfast room.

" Forgive my lack of eloquence," I said to my lady, " and pray believe that I feel more than I can express. If you will promise me the most complete secrecy about all this, and will permit me to make a journey to Paris and in Holland, I will leave to-morrow, and will return in four months to beg you to fulfil intentions which are so honourable and advantageous to me."

" In four months! " said my lady, " and I must promise the most complete secrecy! Why this secrecy, I ask you? Is it to spare the sensibility of that woman? "

" Never mind my motives," I said. " I only engage myself on that condition."

" Do not be angry," said Sir Harry. " Mamma does not know Mistress Caliste."

" I shall marry you, also, my dear Harry, if I marry your mother," I said, embracing him. " I shall really marry you, too, and I swear to you tenderness and fidelity."

" My lady is too reasonable," said my father, " not to consent to the secrecy that you desire; but why not be married in secret before you leave? I should be happy in knowing you married; you could go away as soon as you wished after the ceremony. In this way no suspicion would be aroused, and if there has been any talk, your departure will kill the rumour. I quite understand your desiring to make a journey as a bachelor— that is, without a woman. There was an idea of sending you to travel with your brother, when you left the university, but the war interfered."

Lady Betty was so much appeased by my father's speech that she consented to all he wished, and thought it amusing for us to be married before a certain ball that was to be given in a few days.

" The error in which we see everyone will divert us," she said.

With what speed did I not see myself carried on!
I had known Lady Betty for about five months.
Our marriage was suggested, discussed, and decided
in an hour. Sir Harry was so happy that I had
difficulty in believing that he would be discreet.
He said that four months was too long for him to
keep silence, but that he would say nothing till my
departure if I would promise to take him with me.
I was accordingly married, and nothing became
known, although contrary winds and excessively
stormy weather delayed my departure for some
days, which it was more natural to pass at Bath
than at Harwich. The wind having changed I
departed, leaving Lady Betty with child. In four
months I travelled the principal towns of Holland,
Flanders, and Brabant; and in France, besides
Paris, I saw Normandy and Brittany. I did not
travel fast, on account of my little travelling companion; but I stayed for a short time wherever I
went and nowhere did I desire to remain longer.
I was so ill disposed for society, and what I saw
of women everywhere gave me so little hope of
being consoled for my loss, that I sought only for
edifices, theatrical performances, pictures, and
artists. When I saw or heard anything pleasing
I would look round for her with whom I had for
so long seen and heard, for her with whom I
longed to see and to hear everything, who would
have aided my judgments and doubled my sensibility. I took up my pen a hundred times to
write to her, but I did not dare to write; for how

could I send her such a letter as would have given me any happiness to write or her to receive?

Without little Harry I should have found myself alone even in the most populous towns; with him I was not entirely isolated even in the most retired places. He loved me, he never incommoded me, and I found a thousand ways of causing him to talk of Caliste without speaking of her myself. We returned to England, first to Bath, then to my father; and finally to London, where our marriage was made public as soon as Lady Betty thought it time for her to be presented at the court. People had talked of my brother and me as an example of friendship; they had talked of me as a gallant young man rendered interesting by the passion of an amiable woman. My father's friends had maintained that I should distinguish myself by my knowledge and my talent. Men of culture had praised my taste and sensibility for the arts they themselves professed. In London, in society, only a gloomy and silent man was to be perceived.

The world grew astonished at Caliste's passion and at Lady Betty's choice; and, even supposing that the earlier judgments passed on me were not altogether false, I admit that the later were at least perfectly natural, and gave me but little pain. But Lady Betty, becoming aware of the public opinion, adopted it unconsciously, and, not finding herself as much beloved as she thought she deserved to be, after having complained for some time with considerable vivacity, sought for consolation in a kind of contempt which she nourished and on which she prided herself. I thought none of her impressions so unfair as to be offended by them or able to combat them. Besides, I should not have known how to set about it, and I admit that I did not take a sufficiently lively interest to be either very clear-sighted or very ingenious, and still less to become angry; so she did just as she chose and she chose to please and to shine in society, which her handsome face, her genteel manners, and that gift of repartee that always succeeds in females, made very easy to her. From a general coquetry she passed to one more particular—for I cannot call by any other term that sentiment which inclined her to the man in all England with whom a woman might feel herself the most flattered to be seen, but who was the least capable, or so it seemed to me, of feeling or inspiring passion. . . . I appeared to see nothing and to object to nothing, and, after the birth of her daughter, Lady Betty gave herself up without reserve to all the amusements that fashion and her own taste rendered agreeable to her. As to the little baronet he was well content with me, for I occupied myself almost entirely with him, and the only real sorrow that his mother gave me was her insisting obstinately on his being sent to school at Westminster when, after her lying-in, we went to the country.

It was about that time that my father, having taken me to walk one day at some distance from the house, spoke to me frankly of the manner of life that my lady was leading, and asked me if I did not think I ought to oppose it before it became altogether scandalous. I replied that it was not possible for me to add to my other troubles that of interfering with a person who had given herself to me with more apparent advantages to me than to herself, and who, at bottom, had her own reasons for complaint.

" There is no one," I said, " to whose affections, self-love, and activity some food is not necessary. Women of the people have their domestic cares and their children, with whom they are compelled to occupy themselves a great deal; women of fashion, if they have not a husband to whom they are everything, and who is everything to them, have recourse to gaming, to gallantry, or to devotion. My lady does not care for gaming, besides, she is still too young to game, she is handsome and amiable; that which is happening is too natural to be complained of, and does not touch me nearly enough for me to desire to complain of it. I do not intend to acquire the ill-temper or the absurdity of a jealous husband; if she were rational, serious, capable, in a word, of listening to and crediting me, if there existed between us any true harmony of character, I should perhaps become her friend and should exhort her to avoid publicity and scandal in order to save herself unhappiness and not to alienate public consideration; but, as she would not listen to me, it is better that I should preserve my own dignity and let her remain in ignorance of my indulgence being deliberate. She will commit some imprudences the less if she thinks she is deceiving me. I know all that might be said to me about the evil of tolerating disorder; but I could not prevent it, without never letting my wife out of my sight. Now, what moralist is severe enough to prescribe to me such a task! If it *were* prescribed to me I should refuse to submit, I should let myself be condemned by every authority, and I should invite that man who could say that he himself tolerated no abuse, either in public life, if he were connected with it, or in his home, if he possessed one, or in the conduct of his children, if he had any, or in his own conduct, I should invite that man, I say, to throw the first stone."

My father, seeing me so determined, made no reply. He entered into my point of view and always lived on good terms with Lady Betty; and, during the short time in which we were still together, there was no day on which he did not give me some proof of his extreme affection for me.

I remember that, about that time, a bishop, a relative of Lady Betty's, who was dining at my father's with a large company, began to utter these commonplaces, half moral, half jocose, about marriage, marital authority, etc., which might be called ecclesiastical pleasantries, which belong to all periods, and which, on this occasion, might have had a special aim. After permitting

him to exhaust anew this old subject, I said that it
was for law and religion or for their ministers, to
keep women in order, and that, if husbands were
to be charged with it, there would have at least
to be a dispensation for busy people, who would
then have too much to do, and for soft and indolent folk, who would be made too uneasy. " If they
did not have that indulgence for *us*," I said with
some emphasis, " marriage would only suit busy-
bodies and idiots, Argus, or those who have no
eyes." Lady Betty blushed. I thought to read in
her looks some astonishment at my still retaining
sufficient intelligence to talk in such a way. I only
needed, perhaps, in order to be restored to her
favour at that moment, the preference of some
other pretty woman. An incident, which it is not
worth while to recall, made me suppose this. It
seems that, at bottom, although it does not always
appear, women have great confidence in each
other's taste. A man is a piece of goods, which,
circulating amongst them, increases in value for
some time until he falls suddenly into complete
discredit, a discredit usually only too well-
deserved.

Towards the end of September I returned to
London to see Sir Harry. I hoped also that, being
the only one of our family there at a season when
the town was deserted, I could go everywhere
without being observed and might meet eventually
in a coffee-house, or tavern, someone who could
give me news of Caliste. It was a year and a few

days since we had been parted. If none of my
attempts had succeeded I should have gone to
General D——, or to the old relative who wished
to leave her his fortune. I could no longer
support existence without some knowledge of her
doings; the void she had left in my life affected me
each day more cruelly. People are mistaken in
holding that it is in the first days that we are most
sensible of a great bereavement. It seems at first
as if we were not altogether sure of our misfortune. We are not quite certain that it *is*
without a remedy, and the beginning of the most
cruel separation is only like an absence. But when
the days in passing never bring back the person for
whom we crave, it seems that our unhappiness is
continually confirmed, and, at each moment, we
cry, " It is indeed for ever! "

On the morrow of my arrival in London, after
having passed the day with my little friend, I went
alone in the evening to the play, thinking to muse
more at my ease there than elsewhere. There was
a small assembly even for the time of year, for it
was excessively hot and the sky threatened a storm.
I entered a box and, in my distraction, I thought
myself for some time to be alone. At length I
perceived a lady whose features were concealed
from me by a large hat. She had not turned when
I entered, and appeared lost in the deepest reverie.
Something in her air recalled Caliste; but Caliste,
withdrawn into Norfolk by her husband and of
whom I had heard no word in town up to the

middle of the summer, must, I thought, be so far away that I did not dwell on the thought for an instant. The piece began; it proved to be the *Fair Penitent.* I uttered an exclamation of surprise. The lady turned; it *was* Caliste. Judge of our astonishment, our emotion, our joy! (for every other sentiment gave place in that instant to the joy of meeting). I forgot the faults I had committed, the regrets I had felt; I no longer had a wife or she a husband; we had found each other again; were it but for a few moments we could feel only that.

She appeared to me a little paler and more careless in her dress, but nevertheless more beautiful than I had ever seen her.

"What good fortune!" she said, "what happiness! I had come to see the piece that at this very theatre decided my lot. It is the first time that I have come here since that day. I had never had the courage to return; now other regrets have made me insensible to that kind of shame. I came to evoke my earliest experiences, and to reflect on my life; and it is you whom I find here, you the real, the only interest of my life, the constant object of my thought, of my memory, of my regrets, you, whom I did not dare to hope I should ever see again."

For a long time I did not answer her. For a long time we gazed at each other, as if we each wished to assure ourselves that it was truly the other. "Is it really you?" I said at last. "It is really

you? I came here without design, out of idleness; I should have thought myself happy to have
had only news of you after the many researches
that I proposed to make, and I find you, yourself,
and alone, and we shall have, for at least a few
hours, the happiness that we previously had at
every hour and every day."

Then I begged her to agree that we should
each in turn recount the history of the time that
had passed since our separation, in order that we
might understand one another better and talk
more at our ease. She agreed, told me to begin,
and listened almost without interruption; only,
when I accused myself, she excused me; when I
spoke of her she smiled with feeling; when she
saw me disturbed she looked at me with pity.
The lack of intimacy that was apparent between
Lady Betty and myself did not seem to afford her
pleasure, although she did not affect to feel regret.

"I see," she said, "that I have never been
entirely despised or forgotten; it is as much as I
could ask. I thank you for it, and I give thanks to
God that I have come to know it. I will not tell
you all that I suffered on the journey from Bath
to London, trembling at the least sound I heard
behind me, not daring to look back for fear of
finding it was *not* you; enlightened at length
despite myself, again deluding myself, again
undeceived. . . . That is enough: if you do not
divine all that I might tell you, you would never
comprehend it. On arriving in London I learned

that my father's uncle had died a few days previously, and had left me his fortune, which, with
all the legacies paid, amounted, in addition to his
house, to almost thirty thousand pounds.

" This event affected me, although the death of a
man of eighty is really at each moment less
astonishing than his life, and I felt a sort of regret
of which it took me some time to discover the
cause. I did discover it, however. I had now an
obligation the more not to break my engagement
of marriage. Having before listened to Mr. M——,
to reject him at the moment when I had something
to give in exchange for a name and an honourable
position, appeared to me almost impossible. There
would have accrued to me a kind of dishonour to
which I was not resigned. He arrived the following day, showed me an account of his fortune, as
clear as the fortune itself, and a marriage contract
already drawn up, by which he gave me three
hundred pounds a year during my life and, in
addition, a dowry of five thousand pounds. He
knew nothing of my inheritance; I told him. I
refused the income that he offered me, but I asked
that, supposing our marriage were indeed celebrated (a phrase that I repeated frequently), I
might retain the enjoyment of and exclusive rights
in all that I at present possessed and might in the
future receive from the liberality of Lord L——;
and I begged that I might be considered as absolutely free until the moment that I pronounced the
word ' yes ' at the altar.

" ' You see, sir,' I said, ' how discomposed I am; I desire that, until then, my word shall, so to speak, be counted for nothing, and that you shall give me your word of honour to make me no reproaches if I retract the moment before the ceremony is concluded.'

" ' I swear it,' he said, ' if you change of yourself; but if another comes and causes you to change, I will have his life or he mine. A man who has known you for so long and has not had the courage to do that which I am doing, does not deserve to be preferred to me.'

" After this speech the very thing I had till then so much desired appeared to me the most to be apprehended. He soon returned with the contract altered as I had desired, but he gave me by it five thousand guineas for the jewels, the furniture, and the pictures that belonged to me in my own right. The clergyman was warned, the licence obtained, the witnesses found. I begged for an hour more of solitude and liberty. I wrote to you and gave my letter to my faithful James. No letter came from you. The hour passed, we went to the church, and they married us. . . .

" Let me take breath for a moment," she said, and affected to listen to the actors and the " Caliste " of the theatre, whose performance made the tears, that her neighbours saw her shed, appear sufficiently natural. Then she continued. " Some days later, the business concerning the inheritance being settled, and my husband having taken possession of the property, he carried me to his country seat; the uncle of Lord L—— making me promise, as I took leave of him, to come and see him whenever he desired it. I was perfectly well received in the place which was to be my home. Tenants, friends, neighbours, even the proudest of those who had the most right to be proud, were eager to make me welcome, so that it was in my power to believe that they knew me by favourable report alone. For the first time I permitted myself to doubt whether your father were not mistaken, and if it were quite certain that I should have brought dishonour in my train. I, for my part, neglected nothing which could give pleasure and recompense them for their civility. My old habit of adapting to others my actions, my words, my voice, and my movements, even my countenance itself, came back to me, and served me in such good stead that I venture to affirm that in four months Mr. M—— did not pass a moment which was disagreeable. I never uttered your name; the clothes that I wore, the music that I played were no longer the same as at Bath. I had become two persons, one of whom was only occupied with silencing and concealing the nature of the other. Love (for my husband felt for me a true passion) seconded my efforts by its illusions: he appeared to believe that no one had ever been so dear to me as he was. He certainly deserved all that I did and all that I could have done for his happiness during a long life; but his happiness only endured four months.

"We were seated at the table of one of our

neighbours. A gentleman just arrived from
London talked of a marriage which had been
solemnized some time before, but which had only
recently been made public. He did not at first
recollect the name; but at length he named you.
I said nothing, but I fainted away, and was two
hours in recovering my senses. The next most
terrifying accidents followed each other during
the next few days and ended in a miscarriage of
which the consequences brought me twenty times
to the brink of the grave. I scarcely saw Mr. M——.
A lady who had heard my story and who had pity
on my situation, kept him away from me, in order
that I should not see his sorrow or hear his
reproaches; and, at the same time she neglected
nothing that might serve to console or to appease
him. She did more. I had persuaded myself that
you had been secretly married before I left Bath;
that you had been already engaged before you had
returned there; that you had deceived me in
saying that you did not know Lady Betty, that you
had permitted me to arrange my rival's apartment,
and had made use of me, my zeal, my industry, and
my care in order to pay her your court; that, when
you had shown ill-humour at finding Mr. M——
with me you were already promised, perhaps
already married. This lady, seeing me constantly
preoccupied by these painful conjectures, and
returning perpetually to the most heartrending
ideas, informed herself, without telling me, of the
impression that my departure had made on you,

of your father's behaviour, of the date of your marriage and that of your departure, delayed by bad weather, and of your behaviour during your journey and after your return. She was able to fathom everything, and to make both your servants and Sir Harry's speak; and her information was very exact, for that which you have just told me corresponds with it to perfection. I was consoled, and thanked her over and over again, weeping and kissing her hands, which I moistened with my tears. Alone, at night, I used to say to myself, ' At least I need not despise or hate him; I was not the plaything of a plot, of a premeditated betrayal. He did not make a toy of my love and my blindness.' I was, I say, consoled, and I recovered sufficient health to return to my usual life, hoping to cause my husband to forget, by dint of attentions and consideration, the painful impression that he had received. In this I was not successful. Estrangement, if not hate itself, had taken the place of love. I still interested him, however, whenever a return of my malady appeared to threaten my life; but, as soon as I was better, he fled the house, and when, on his return to it, he perceived her who so brief a time before had made it delightful to him, I used to see him shudder. For three months I combated this unhappy humour, and this much more for his sake than for my own. Always alone, or with the lady who had come to my aid, working incessantly for him or for his house, neither writing nor receiving letters, my sadness, my humiliation (for his friends had all abandoned me) would, I thought, have power to touch him; but he was hopelessly embittered. No word of reproach ever escaped him, so that I never had the opportunity of saying a single one of excuse or justification. Once or twice I attempted to speak, but I found it impossible to utter a word. At length, having received a letter from the General, who told me that he was ill and asked me to go and see him either alone or with Mr. M——, I placed it before my husband. 'You may go, madam,' he said.

"I departed the following day, leaving Fanny behind me, in order not to produce the appearance of deserting the house or of being banished from it, and bidding her leave my wardrobes and drawers open to the inspection of anyone. But I do not think he deigned to examine anything or to put the least question concerning me. That is how the woman whom my lord loved so well, and whom you once loved, returned to London! To-day I find myself here more unhappy and neglected than when I played in this theatre and belonged only to a mother who bartered me for money."

Caliste did not weep after having finished her story; she appeared to be considering her fate with a kind of astonishment mixed with horror, rather than with sadness. But I remained sunk in the most sombre reflections.

"Do not distress yourself," she said smiling; "I am not worth it. I knew very well that the

end would not be happy, and I have had such
sweet moments! The joy of finding you again
would make up for a century of suffering. What
am I, after all, but a kept woman, whom you
honoured more than she deserved?" And with a
tranquil voice and manner she began to ask for
news of Sir Harry, and if he was fond of his little
sister.

I spoke to her of her own health.

"I am not well," she said, "and I do not think
that I shall ever recover, but I realize that it will
take a long time for a good constitution to be
entirely destroyed by sorrow."

We spoke a little of the future. Ought she not
to try to go to Norfolk, where duty alone, without
any attraction, any inclination, any hope of
happiness, would take her? Should she ask Lord
L——'s uncle to conduct her to spend the winter
in France? If she and I both passed the winter in
London could we see each other, or could we bear
not to see each other?

At the end of the play we went out without
having come to any agreement, without knowing
where we were going, without thinking either of
separating, of meeting again, or of remaining
together. The sight of James raised me from this
state of complete oblivion.

"Ah, James!" I cried.

"Ah, sir, is it you? By what chance, what
good fortune . . .? Wait! I will call a coach
instead of this chair."

Thus it was James who decided that I should remain for a few more minutes with Caliste.

" Where do you desire to go? " he asked.

" To St. James's Park," she said, after having glanced at me.

" Let us be together for a moment longer; no one will know. It is the first secret that James has ever had to keep for me; I am sure that he will not betray it. And if you wish that the reports of those who may have seen us at the play should not be believed, or that no attention should be paid to this meeting, go back to the country to-night or to-morrow; people will think that you must have been quite indifferent to finding me again, since you depart at once."

It is thus that even a little happiness brings back the love of propriety, the care for the peace of mind of others, to a noble and generous soul.

" But write to me," she added. " Advise me, tell me your plans. There is now no objection to my occasionally receiving letters from you."

I agreed to everything. I promised both to go away and to write.

We arrived at the gates of the park. It was very dark and it began to thunder.

" Are you not alarmed? " I asked.

" Let it kill only me," she said, " and all would be well. But if it is better not to go far away from the gate and the carriage, let us sit down on this bench."

Then, after having looked at the sky for a little

time, " Certainly no one will be out walking," she
said, " no one will hear or see us."

With trembling fingers she cut a lock of my
hair and placed it in her bosom; then, putting
both her arms around me, she said, " What shall
we do without each other? In half an hour I shall
be as I was a year ago, as six months ago, as this
morning: what shall I do if I still have some time
to live? Shall we go away together? Have you
not obeyed your father sufficiently? Have you not
a wife and child of his choosing? Let us return to
our real ties. Whom should we injure? My
husband hates and will not live with me; your
wife no longer loves you! . . . No! do not
answer me," she cried, putting her hand over my
mouth, " do not refuse, but do not either consent.
Until now I have only been unhappy; let me not
become guilty! I could support my own guilt but
not yours; I should never forgive myself for
having degraded you! Oh, how unhappy I am,
and how I love you! Never was any man so
beloved as you! " And, holding me in a close
embrace, she burst into a flood of tears.

" I am an ungrateful wretch," she said a moment
later. " I am ungrateful to say I am unhappy; I
would not exchange for anything in the world the
happiness that I have had to-day, the happiness
that I still am having."

The thunder had become terrifying and the sky
seemed as if on fire. Caliste appeared to see and to
hear nothing; but James, running up, cried: " In

heaven's name, madam, come! Here is the hail. You have been so ill." And taking her by the arm, as soon as he could perceive her, he drew her towards the coach, made her enter it, and closed the door. I remained alone in the darkness. I never saw her again.

The following morning, very early, I returned to the country. My father, surprised by my return, and by the agitation in which he saw me, put me some friendly questions. He had acquired a right to my confidence, and I told him everything.

"In your place," he said, "but this is not speaking as a father—in your place I do not know what I should do. 'Let us return,' she said, 'to our real ties.' Was she right? But she did not wish it herself. . . . It was only in a moment of frenzy from which she quickly recovered. . . ."

I was pacing up and down the gallery in which we were conversing. My father was leaning on a table, his head buried in his hands; the sound of voices put an end to the strange scene.

My lady was coming back from a hunting party: she was apparently apprehensive of something vexatious from my speedy return, for she changed colour on seeing me; but I passed close to her and her friends without saying anything to them. I had only just sufficient time to dress myself before dinner, and I appeared at table with my accustomed air. All that I saw indicated to me that my lady was happy in my absence, and that her husband's

unexpected return did not suit her at all. My
father was so much struck by this that upon our
rising from table he said to me, pressing my hand
with as much bitterness as pity, " Oh why did I
take you away from Caliste? But why did you
not make her known to me? Who could have
believed that there should be so much difference
between one woman and another, and that one
should have loved you with so constant and true a
passion! "

Seeing me enter my room he followed me, and
we remained for a space seated opposite to each
other without a word. The sound of wheels made
us look towards the avenue. It was Lord N——,
the father of the young man with whom you have
seen me. He came straight up to me and said:
" See if you can, if you will, do me a great
service. I have an only son whom I wish to send
travelling. He is very young; I cannot accompany
him because my wife cannot leave her father and
would die of anxiety and tedium were she to be
at the same time deprived of both her son and her
husband. As I say, my son is very young, and yet
I would rather send him to travel alone than
confide him to anyone but you. You are not on
very good terms with your wife, my son is
amiable, the expenses of the journey would be
shared. Think it over. As I find you with your
father I shall only allow you a quarter of an hour
for reflection."

I glanced at my father; he drew me aside.

" Consider this, my son," he said, " as a providential means of escape from your own weakness and mine. She who is, so to speak, driven away by her husband and is the delight of an old man, her benefactor, in London, can safely remain there. I shall lose you, but I have deserved to do so. You will be of use to another father and to a young man of whom much is hoped; that is a consolation which I shall endeavour to appreciate."

" I will go," I said, returning to my lord, " but on two conditions, which I will tell you, after I have taken a breath of fresh air."

" I agree to them beforehand," he said, clasping my hand, " and I thank you. Consider it settled."

My two conditions were, the one that we should begin by Italy, in order that I should not during our stay there have as yet lost any of my authority over the young man; the other, that, after a year, whether satisfied or dissatisfied with him, I should be able to leave him whenever I desired without disobliging his parents.

That same evening I wrote to Caliste all that had occurred. I insisted upon her replying to me, and I promised to continue to write to her.

" Let us not deny ourselves," I said, " an innocent pleasure, the only one which remains to us."

I was of opinion that we had better make the journey by sea, in order to have an experience the more. We embarked at Plymouth. We disembarked at Lisbon. From there we went by land to Cadiz, and then by sea to Messina, where we saw the horrid traces of the earthquake. I remember, madam, to have already told you all this in detail, and you also are aware how, after a year's stay in Italy, crossing the Saint-Gothard pass, and seeing in Valois the glaciers, baths, and salt springs, we found ourselves at the beginning of the winter at Lausanne, where a certain likeness attached me to you, where your house became a refuge to me, and your kindness a consolation. I have now only to tell you about my unhappy Caliste.

I received her reply to my letter just before sailing. She lamented her fate, but she approved my resolution and my journey, and prayed that it would be fortunate. She also wrote to my father to thank him for his compassion, and to ask his forgiveness for any sorrow she might have caused him.

The winter came. Lord L——'s uncle did not make a good recovery from his gout, and she decided to remain in London. He was indeed seriously ill for some time, and she often passed her days and portions of her nights in nursing him. When he was better he attempted to entertain her and to enliven himself by inviting to his house men of the first society in London. There were big dinners and rather noisy suppers, after which gaming often went on far into the night; and he liked Caliste to grace the assembly until it broke up.

At other times he pressed her to go into society,

telling her that complete retirement would bear the appearance of her having called down on herself her husband's disfavour, and that Mr. M—— himself would judge her more favourably if he heard that she dared to show herself and was everywhere well received. All these varied exertions were too much for one whose health, after having suffered a severe shock, was unceasingly undermined by sorrow (I must be forgiven for saying this with a kind of pride for which I pay sufficiently dearly), by sorrow, and by the continual regret of being without me. Her letters, filled always with the tenderest feeling, left me no doubt as to the unfailing constancy of her attachment. Towards the spring she wrote me one which gave me at once a great deal of pleasure and the acutest pain.

" I was at the play yesterday," she wrote, " and had reserved for myself a place in the same box as in September. I think that my good angel must inhabit that place. Scarcely was I seated when I heard a young voice exclaim: ' Oh! there is dear Mrs. Caliste! But how thin she has grown! Look at her now, sir. Your son never took you to her, but you can see her now.'

" It was your father who was addressed. He bowed to me with a look which I must not try to describe to you if I desire my eyes to serve me in writing this; it would be equally difficult to portray for you all his countenance conveyed of goodness, tenderness, and sadness.

246

" ' But what have you done to get so thin? ' asked Sir Harry.

" ' Many things, my child,' I said. ' But you, you have grown and look as if you had always been well and happy.'

" ' I am, however, vastly put out,' he said, ' not to be with our friend in Italy; and it seems to me that I had more right to be with him than his cousin had. But I have always suspected that mamma did not wish it, for it was she also who insisted that I should be sent to Westminster; as to him, he would willingly have kept me and offered to give me all my lessons, which would have been far pleasanter for me than Westminster school; and we might have often talked of you. It is so long since I have seen you that I must now talk to you freely you know; I have often thought that my having loved you so much and having been so sad at your departure did not do me much good with mamma; but I must not say any more about that, for she is looking at me from the opposite box and might guess, from my air, what I was saying.'

" You can imagine the effect of these words. I did not dare, on account of Lady Betty's gaze, to have recourse to my smelling bottle, but I could scarcely breathe.

" ' But at least you are not pale,' said Sir Harry, ' and I dare to hope, on that account, that you are not ill.'

" ' That is because I am wearing rouge,' I said.

" ' But eighteen months ago you used not to wear it! '

" At length your father told him to leave me a little in peace, and, a few moments later, inquired if I had news of you, and told me the contents of your laſt letters to himself. I was able to remain in my place till the firſt interval, but the observation of your wife and of those who accompanied her, always fixed upon me, at length compelled me to go out.

" Sir Harry ran to call my chair and your father had the goodness to conduƈt me to it."

About the month of June Caliſte, I learned, was advised to take asses' milk. The General wished her to take it at home, feeling assured that she only had to show herself to the man whom he had seen so passionately in love with her for him to recover the sentiments that she deserved to inspire.

" It is I," he said, " who, in a manner, was the cause of your marriage; I will take you back to your home, and we shall see whether they dare to receive you ill."

Caliſte obtained his permission to warn her husband, but not to await his reply. On her arrival she found this letter:

" The General is perfeƈtly in the right, madam, and you have done well to return home. Endeavour to recover your health, and consider yourself as completely miſtress here. I have given the moſt definite orders to this effeƈt, although there was no

need, for my servants are yours. I have loved you
too much, and I esteem you too highly, not to hope
to yet live happily with you; but at present, the
impression of the sorrow that I have felt is still too
keen and, in spite of myself, I should let you see it
too much. I am about to make, in order to try to
efface it completely, a journey of some months,
of which I hope all the more success as I have
never as yet quitted my own country. You will
not be able to write to me, as you will not know
where to address your letters, but I shall write to
you, and people will see that we are not estranged.
Farewell, madam; it is very sincerely that I desire
your better health, and that I regret having shown
so much chagrin over an involuntary action and
one which you have made so many efforts to repair.
But my suffering was too acute. Show much
kindness to Mrs. H——. She has truly deserved
it, and I can now do her justice. I was not then
able to believe that there had been no secret
correspondence, no intercourse between you and
the fortunate man to whom your heart was given;
she used to tell me in vain that your astonishment
was the proof of this, but I heeded nothing."

Mr. M——'s departure had produced more
effect than his commands, and Caliste was at first
none too well received. But her protector took so
haughty a tone and she showed so much sweetness
and was so good and benevolent, so just and so
dignified, that everyone was soon at her feet, her
neighbours as much as the household. And, what

is not usual with friends in the country, they were as discreet as they were zealous, so that she was able to take her milk with all the care and tranquillity that others could procure for her. She wrote to me that she was deriving some benefit from it, and that people began to think her improved. But, in the midst of her cure, the General fell ill with the prolonged malady of which he died. She was compelled to return to London; and fatigue, watching, and sorrow struck her a violent and final blow. Her faithful friend, protector, and benefactor gave her, in dying, the capital of six hundred pounds a year in the three per cents., from the safest portion of his fortune, to be estimated by his legal advisers. After his death she went at first to reside in his mansion at Whitehall, which, during the preceding winter, she had already amused herself by putting in order. She continued to receive Lord L——'s and his uncle's friends, and permitted herself every week the indulgence of hearing the best musicians of London—that is almost to say, of Europe. I learned all this from herself. She told me also that she had given a home to a singer of light opera who had tired of the theatre, and had afforded her the means of marrying a musician who was also a very respectable man. " I make use of them," she said, " in order to teach some music to little orphans, whom I myself am instructing, and whom I am having taught a profession. When I am told that I am breeding these children up to be courtesans, I observe that I take them very young and very pretty, which, in a town like London, leads to an almost certain and complete degradation, and the danger is not increased by their knowing how to sing a little; I have even dared to say that it would, after all, be better to commence and to end as I have done than to go on the streets, and to die in a hospital. They sing the choruses of 'Esther' and 'Athalie,' which I have had translated and for which the most beautiful music has been written. This entertains me, and it is their principal recreation."

All these details could not, you will admit, madam, prepare me for this terrible letter which I received eight days ago. Return it to me in order that it may never leave me again until my own death.

" At last, my friend, can I say to you that *it is over*. Yes; *it is over* for ever. I must bid you an eternal farewell. I will not recount to you the symptoms which have given me warning of a speedy end; it would be to fatigue myself uselessly, but it is quite certain that I am not deceiving either you or myself. Your father came to visit me yesterday; I was deeply touched by this kindness. He said to me ' If in the spring, madam, if in the spring ' (he could not bring himself to add ' if you are still living ') ' I will, myself, attend you to France, to Nice, or to Italy. My son is at present in Switzerland; I will tell him to come and meet us.'

" ' It is too late, sir,' I said to him, ' but I am nevertheless touched by your kindness.'

" He said nothing further, but it was out of consideration for me, for he was assuredly feeling much that he would have desired to express. I asked for news of your daughter, and he told me that she was well and that he would already have sent her to me if she had at all resembled you, but that, although she was only eighteen months old, it was already apparent that she was to take after her mother. I asked him to send me Sir Harry, and said that I would have conveyed him by the boy a present that I did not myself dare to make him. He said that he would receive with pleasure from my own hands anything that I desired to give him; whereupon I gave him your portrait, which you sent me from Italy. I will give Sir Harry the copy that I have made of it, but I shall myself keep the first portrait that you gave me, and will say that it is to be returned to you after my death.

" I have not made you happy, and I am leaving you unhappy, and I myself am dying; yet I cannot bring myself to wish that I had never known you, and even if I ought to reproach myself, I cannot do it. Yet the last moment in which I saw you has sometimes come back to my mind, and I have feared that there was a certain audacity in our complete heedlessness of the danger that threatened us both. That, perhaps, is what is called defying Providence; yet is it possible for an atom, a grain of dust, to defy the Supreme Being, dare

we even cherish such a thought? and, even supposing that in a moment of frenzy man *should*
forget God and His judgments, could the Al-
mighty therefore be angry? Farewell, my friend;
write to me that you have received this letter.
Write me just a few words; there is but little
probability of their finding me still alive, but if I *do*
live to receive them I shall enjoy once again the
happiness of seeing your hand."

Since that letter, madam, I have received nothing.
"It is too late," she said, "it is too late." Oh,
unhappy man that I am! I have always waited
until it was too late, and so did my father. If she
had loved another man, and he had had another
father, she would have lived; she would not have
perished from grief. . . .

LETTER XXII

(From the same to the same)

MADAM,

I have not received any further letters. There
are moments when I still venture to hope. But no;
that is not true. I no longer hope. I already think
of her as dead, and I am heartbroken. I had
become accustomed to her illness as I was to her
goodness, as I was to being her lover. I did not
believe that she would marry; I did not believe
that she would die; and now I must endure what

I had not the courage to foresee. Before the last blow had fallen, or, rather, before I *know* that it has fallen, I will make use of what fortitude remains to me to tell you something which is perhaps of no importance, but which I feel myself compelled to relate. During several days devoted wholly to my memories, which the narration to you has turned into living facts, I conversed with no one, not even with my lord. But this morning, when he came to inquire how I had rested, I pressed his hand and, instead of replying to his question, I said, "My boy, if ever it happens to you to touch the heart of a woman who is truly tender and filled with sensibility, and you do not feel in your heart that you can repay her tenderness and her devotion, remove yourself from her, make her forget you, or remember that you may be exposing her to innumerable sorrows and yourself to terrible and eternal regrets."

He remained, pensive, at my side, and, an hour later, recalling to my mind what I had one day said of the various reasons that your daughter might have for not continuing to live with us in a kind of retreat, he asked if I thought she had felt a preference for someone. I replied that I had suspected it. He asked if it had been for him. I answered that I had sometimes thought so.

"If that be so," he said, "it is a sad pity that Miss Cecilia should be so well-born; for to *marry* at my age is not to be thought of."

But again, this may mean nothing. I never

thought or said anything similar; I should at any moment have preferred Caliste as much to my liberty as to a throne; and yet what have I done for her? While people frequently do everything for someone for whom they *think* they would do nothing.

What interest can you feel, madam, in the fate of a man who is certainly the most unhappy in the world, but who also most deserves his unhappiness! I see myself constantly as I was, without, however, being able to understand myself. I do not know if all those wretches who have gradually sunk from the position where fortune had placed them are like me; if so, I do indeed pity them. It appears to me that I did nothing of that which was natural to do. I ought to have married her without asking for a permission of which I had no need. I ought to have prevented her from promising not to marry me without that permission. If all my efforts were not able to move my father I ought to have made her my mistress—for herself and for me really my wife—when her whole heart longed for that, and I perceived it, in spite of all that she said. I ought to have heeded her when, that last evening, alone with me, she

attempted to prevent my leaving her. When I
returned that evening I ought to have forced her
door; and, the next day, have compelled her to
see me, or at least have followed her when she
escaped me. I ought to have remained free, and
not have caused her the unhappiness of believing
that her place was filled beforehand, that she had
been betrayed, or that she was forgotten. Having
found her again I ought never to have left her, I
ought to have been at least as prompt, as zealous
as her faithful James; perhaps I ought not to have
let her leave that coach alone, perhaps James
would have concealed me somehow near her,
perhaps I might have served her together with
him; (I was not known to anyone in her benefactor's house). And even this autumn . . . this
winter. . . .

I knew that her husband had left her; why did
I not, instead of dreaming of her at your chimney
corner, go to nurse her protector with her, relieve
his suffering, and share her watches; compel her
to live, by dint of tenderness and care, or at least,
in reward of her long and devoted passion, give
her the pleasure of seeing me in dying, of seeing
that she had not loved an insensible automaton,
and that, even if I had not known how to love her
as she deserved, I yet knew how to weep for her!
But it is too late; my regret even has come too
late, and she remains in ignorance of it. She
remained in ignorance of it, I should say; I must
at least summon the fortitude to believe her dead,

for, if there had been any return of hope she would have endeavoured to soften the impression of her letter; for she, *she* knew how to love. . . . Behold me therefore alone on earth! She who loved me is no more. I was without the courage to foresee this loss; I am now without the firmness to endure it.

LETTER XXIV

(From my Lord E. to Mme. de C.)

MADAM,

Having learned that you propose to depart to-morrow I hoped to have the honour of visiting you to-day, in order to wish you, together with Mademoiselle Cecilia, a prosperous journey, and to tell you that my regret in seeing you go is only softened by the confidence that I cherish of meeting you both again; but I cannot leave my relative; the impression made upon him by a letter which arrived this morning has been so overwhelming that M. Tissot has absolutely prohibited either me or his servant from leaving him. He who brought him the letter does not leave him either, but he is almost as distressed as is my relative, and would, I think, be more likely to kill himself than to hinder my cousin's doing so. I beg you, madam, to retain for me the kind sentiments of which I have felt the value more than you, perhaps, believe, and for which my gratitude will end only with my life.

I have the honour to be, etc.,

EDWARD ———

LETTER XXV

(From Mr. M. (the husband of Caliſte) to Mr. William D.)

She who so much loved you died yeſterday evening. To speak of her in this manner is no reproach; I had forgiven her a long time since, and indeed, at bottom, she had never injured me. It is true that she did not open her heart to me; I do not know if she ought to have done so, and, in truth, if she *had* opened it, it is not certain that I should not, equally, have married her; for I loved her with passion. She was the moſt amiable and, I may add, to my eyes and in my heart, the only amiable woman that I have ever known. If she did not confide in me, neither did she deceive me; I deceived myself. You had not married her; was it credible that, loving you, she had not desired or been able to make you decide to marry her? You know doubtless how cruelly I was undeceived; and although I now repent of having shown so much resentment and chagrin, I cannot, even now, be surprised that, losing at once the conviction of being loved and the hope of having a child by her, I proved lacking in moderation. Fortunately, it is certain that it is not that which killed her. It is certainly not I who am the cause of her death, and, although I have been jealous of you, I prefer at present to be in my place than in yours. Nothing however proves that you have any reproaches to make yourself, and I beg you not to attach that meaning to my words. You would think me, and with reason, impertinent and unjust as well as cruel, for I conceive you also to be profoundly distressed.

On the same day that Mrs. Caliste wrote you her last letter she wrote to me begging me to visit her. I went, without an instant's delay; I found her house arranged like that of a person in good health, and she herself fairly well in appearance, except for her excessive thinness. I was very glad to be able to say to her that she did not appear to me to be as ill as she believed; but she said to me, in smiling, that I was deceived by a little red that she had put on that morning, and which had already spared Fanny some tears and James some sighs. I saw in the evening the little girls that she was bringing up; they sang and she accompanied them on the organ; it was very moving music and much like what I had heard in several churches in Italy. The next morning they sang some more hymns of the same kind; that music closed and opened each day. Then Mrs. Caliste read me her Will, begging me, if I desired her to alter anything, to say so freely; but I found nothing to change. She gave her fortune to the poor, in this manner;

the half—that is to say, the capital of three hundred pounds a year—to be in perpetuity in the hands of the Lord Mayor of London, for the purpose of teaching to three little boys, to be chosen each year from the Foundling Hospital, the trade of pilot, of carpenter, and of cabinet-maker. The first of these professions, she said, was to be chosen by the boldest, the second by the most robust, the third by the most skilful. The other half of her fortune was to be in the hands of the Bishop of London, who was, each year, to take two girls from the Magdalen Hospital, and to place them in partnership with well-established tradeswomen, giving to each of them a hundred and fifty pounds to put into the business in which they were to become partners. She recommended this foundation to the sympathy and goodness of the bishop, his wife, and his relatives. Of the five thousand pounds which I had given her she only wished to dispose of a thousand in Fanny's favour and five hundred in James's, although her uncle's fortune, which she brought me by marriage, was worth at least thirty-five thousand pounds. She begged me to keep Fanny in my service, saying that, by doing so, I would honour herself as well as a girl who deserved esteem, and who, having never served her in anything that was not honest, ought not to be suspected of the contrary. She gave her clothes and her jewels to Mrs. G—— of Norfolk, her house in Bath and everything in it to Sir Harry. She desired that, when her funeral was paid for,

her ready money and the rest of her income for this
year should be divided in equal portions between
the little girls and the servants whom she had, in
addition to James and Fanny. Having assured
herself that there was nothing in this will which
pained me, or was contrary to the law, she made
me promise to have it punctually executed. After
that she continued to live her ordinary life so far as
her strength, which declined daily, permitted; and
we had more talk together than we had ever before
had. In truth, sir, I would have given everything
that I owned in the world to preserve her, to keep
her alive, even in the state in which I had found
her, and to pass the remainder of my days at her
side.

Many people would not believe her as ill as
she was and continued sending her, as they had
done all the winter, copies of verse addressed to
her, sometimes under the name of Caliste, sometimes under that of Aspasia; but she no longer
read them. One day I spoke to her of the pleasure
that she must feel at seeing herself esteemed by
everyone. She assured me that, having been
formerly very sensible of scorn, she had never
become so of esteem. " My judges," she said,
" are only men and women, that is to say, what I
am myself; and I know myself better than they
can know me. The only praise that has given me
pleasure was that of Lord L——'s uncle. He
loved me as being such a person as, according to
him, one ought to be, and if he had had to alter

that opinion it would have greatly disturbed him.
I should have been as sorry as to have died before
him. He had need in some ways that I should live,
and need, also, of esteeming me."

No one ever watched her at night. I wished to
sleep in her room, but she said that it would
trouble her. Fanny's bed was only separated from
hers by a partition that opened without effort or
noise; at the least movement Fanny awoke and
gave her mistress something to drink. During the
last nights I took her place, not because she complained of being too often awakened, but because
the poor girl could no longer hear the weakened
voice, the shortened breathing, without bursting
into tears. It did not certainly pain me less than
her, but I commanded myself better. The day
before yesterday, although Mrs. Caliste was more
oppressed and agitated than usual, she wished to
have her habitual Wednesday concert; but she was
not able to sit at the harpsichord. She caused to
be played for her pieces from Handel's " Messiah,"
from a " Miserere " that had been sent her from
Italy, and from Pergolini's " Stabat Mater."
During an interval she took a ring from her
finger and gave it to me. Afterwards she called
James, gave him a box which she had taken from
her pocket, and said to him:

" Take it to him yourself and, if possible,
remain with him; it is the place, tell him James,
that I had long desired for myself. I should have
been content with it."

After remaining for some moments with her hands clasped and her eyes raised to heaven, she sank down in her chair and closed her eyes. I asked her, seeing that she was very weak, if she wished the music to cease; she made a sign to the contrary and recovered enough strength to thank me for what she called my kindness. The piece over the musicians went out on tiptoe, thinking that she slept; but her eyes had closed for ever.

Thus ended your Caliste, some will say as a pagan, others as a saint; but the lamentations of her servants, the tears of the poor, the consternation of the whole neighbourhood, and the sorrow of a husband who had once believed himself injured, show better than any words what Caliste was.

In thus forcing myself, sir, to give you this melancholy detail, I have considered myself as in some degree pleasing and obeying her; and from the same motive, from the same tender respect to her memory, if I cannot assure you of my friendship, I can, at least, renounce all sentiments of ill-will.

J. M.

THE END

LONDON : CHARLES WHITTINGHAM AND GRIGGS (PRINTERS), LTD.
CHISWICK PRESS, TOOKS COURT, CHANCERY LANE.